A Rogue's SCANDALOUS *Wish*

The Honorable Rogues®, Book Three

COLLETTE CAMERON

Blue Rose Romance®
Portland, Oregon

Sweet-to-Spicy Timeless Romance®

A ROGUE'S SCANDALOUS WISH
The Honorable Rogues®, Book Three
Copyright © 2016 Collette Cameron
Cover Design by: Darlene Albert

Attn: Permissions Coordinator
Blue Rose Romance®
8420 N Ivanhoe # 83054
Portland, Oregon 97203

eBook ISBN: 9781954307438
Paperback ISBN: 9781954307445
www.collettecameron.com

"Shouldn't you be inside dancing, or seducing, or doing whatever handsome, privileged men do at these affairs?"

"Beautiful chemistry...You'll cheer for these star-crossed lovers."

Christi Gladwell USA Today Bestselling Author

Other Collette Cameron Books

The Honorable Rogues®
A Kiss for a Rogue
A Bride for a Rogue
A Rogue's Scandalous Wish
To Capture a Rogue's Heart
The Rogue and the Wallflower
A Rose for a Rogue

Check out Collette's Other Series
Castle Brides
Highland Heather Romancing a Scot
Daughters of Desire (Scandalous Ladies)
The Blue Rose Regency Romances:
The Culpepper Misses
Seductive Scoundrels
Heart of a Scot

Collections
Lords in Love
The Honorable Rogues® Books 1-3
The Honorable Rogues® Books 4-6
Seductive Scoundrels Series Books 1-3
Seductive Scoundrels Series Books 4-6
The Blue Rose Regency Romances-
The Culpepper Misses Series 1-2

Dedication

I lost a beloved grandmother, a step-grandfather, and

foster brother in two separate house fires.

I humbly dedicate this book to

burn victims everywhere.

Bless you!

Acknowledgements

I must give a shout out to Victoria Vane for arranging the photo shoot that allowed me to purchase the amazing cover model image, and also to Darlene Albert for the fabulous cover. Neither can I ignore my faithful beta readers and ARC reviewers. Thank you!

xoxo

Collette

1

Wimpleton's Ball, London, England
Late May 1818

One, two, three, four ... No, I think there are actually five.

Yawning behind her partially open fan, Philomena peeked through the leaves of the enormous cage-shaped potted ficus and counted the wiry hairs sprouting from Lady Clutterbuck's chin. The chinwag and her cronies gossiped a short distance away, their unending litany contributing to the onset of Philomena's nagging headache.

She relaxed a fraction. No sign of Mr. Wrightly, a repugnant would-be suitor, and the reason she'd dove behind the plant when she spied him looking for her earlier.

Pressing two fingertips between her eyes to ease the thrumming there, she located the mantle clock and breathed out a soft sigh. Not yet ten o'clock. She allowed a droll smile. Giles wouldn't consider leaving before the supper dance.

No indeed.

Your brother is determined to find you a husband before Season's end, Philomena Martha Elizabeth Pomfrett. Whether you like it or not.

And she most emphatically did not.

Despite her lack of interest, or the cost to his already fragile health, dear Giles dutifully escorted her to event after event, evening after evening. And she obediently—well, more aptly, reluctantly—husband-hunted.

Content to become a spinster, the mercenary process conflicted with her principles and put her out of sorts, but Giles's time ran short so, for his sake, she pressed onward. Fear of her prospective husband's reaction to her scars created a permanent knot in her belly, and she swallowed against the dryness in her mouth.

Enough.

She shoved the worry aside. She'd deal with that obstacle when the time came. First she had to acquire a spouse, and her prospects weren't altogether promising.

"Oh, would you look at that delicious specimen of manhood." The lascivious tone of Lady Clutterbuck's cohort was entirely inappropriate for an aged, married peeress. "Utterly Scrumptious. Do you know who *he* is?"

The dame actually licked her lips, and thrust her bosoms skyward. Considering her breasts' monstrous size, they barely lifted above her ample waist, and a mere moment later, breathing heavily, she sagged into her former sack-shaped posture.

What unfortunate gentleman had found himself the target of the peeress's lewd attention *this* evening?

"Bradford, Viscount Kingsley. He's just come into his title. One hopes he proves himself worthy of the honor and avoids associating with inferiors and underlings." Lady Clutterbuck's strident voice plowed into Philomena with the force of a winter gale. The dame jutted her superior nose into the air. "That's become so common of late with all the mushrooms and nabobs thinking to force their way into Polite Society. Deep pockets are no substitute for good breeding, I say."

Bradford? Here?

Philomena craned her neck to see around the blasted plant.

Where?

Breath held, she deftly parted the foliage and bent forward.

There, at the ballroom's entrance in his formal evening attire, looking every bit the gentleman of re-finement with his lovely auburn-headed sister, Olivia, on one arm and the distinguished Duchess of Daventry on the other. Unable to deny the giddiness seeing him again brought, fleeting excitement filled Philomena.

He swept the room with his brilliant, blue-eyed—slightly bored—gaze, and she jerked backward, kick-ing the container as she tumbled into the wall.

He can't see you, ninny.

The gossips snapped curious, somewhat distracted glances in her direction.

Drat it all.

She dropped into a crouch with only her forehead visible above the blue and white porcelain, and in a moment, they put their graying heads together and launched into another round of *on dit*. For the first time, Philomena gave thanks that rumors dominated their narrow, peevish minds.

Peering between the ficus's woven branches, she bit her lip as her stomach toppled over itself. She wasn't ready to see Bradford. Face tanned, his raven hair glistening in the candlelight, he threw back his head and laughed at something the duchess said.

How could he have grown even more beautiful? Deucedly unfair to womanhood.

Still squatting, she pivoted right, and then shuffled left. Where was Giles? He'd promised her a beverage several minutes ago. He was nowhere to be seen, at least not from this awkward position.

Most likely, he'd gotten snared in a conversation with another hard-of-hearing matron. That's what came of exploiting their distant connection to the Dowager Marchioness Middleton in order to introduce Philomena to Polite Society.

Not one of the ladies in the dame's favored circle boasted a birthday less than five and seventy years ago, and inevitably, a matron or two or three, imposed upon him to fetch a ratafia, escort her to the card room, retrieve a wrap, or some other trivial matter. Kindhearted, Giles had never been able to politely make his excuses, so he amiably did as they bid.

Half the time, the old birds didn't need what they requested. They just enjoyed a handsome young man's attention for a few moments.

Biting her lower lip, Philomena braved another glance to the ballroom's entrance. Bradford had disappeared into the crowd as well.

Good. She could make her escape.

A cramp seized her calf as she moved to rise. Curses. Closing her eyes, she gripped the pot's edge, waiting for the spasm to pass. Pray God no one came upon her hugging the pottery. Rather hard to explain her sudden rapt interest in dirt and greeneries.

Easing upright, she surreptitiously examined those nearest her. No one had noticed her. Pretty much a testament to her entire dismal Season. An incomparable, she was not.

Ah, here came Giles now, bearing a glass of ratafia in one hand and punch in the other. His limp had become more pronounced, and his countenance more wan, than it had been scarcely twenty minutes ago. Nonetheless, despite the ravages of ill-health, his striking visage turned many a fair maid's head as he ambled toward her hiding place.

Why did he insist on putting them through this every night?

He wants to make certain you are provided for when ...

She blinked away the familiar prickle of tears and the accompanying rush of anger. His delicate heart could fail at any moment. The injustice galled. He should be strong and healthy, seeking a spouse himself, not gravely weakened by a prolonged fever and resigned to an early death.

How she wished there'd been no need for him to

enlist, wished he hadn't been stationed in the West Indies, hadn't been wounded, had received proper treatment. Hadn't contracted Scarlet Fever.

If wishes were horses, beggars would ride.

Forcing composure, Philomena schooled her features into pleasant lines. She would bear her grief with quiet dignity.

His forehead furrowed, Giles peered about in search of her.

Eager to intercept him, and grateful to be spared overhearing more of Lady Clutterbuck's malicious claptrap, Philomena skirted the pot and, after edging along the wall a few feet, stepped out into the open.

Perhaps he would consider joining her in a game of loo or whist. His resting a spell at the card tables would also spare her another partnerless set or two. Blasted hard to acquire a husband when she spent most dances tapping her toes or pretending absorption in cornices, portraits, and elaborately painted ceiling panels.

"There you are." Passing her the ratafia, Giles grinned and winked, his gray-green eyes, so like hers, glinting with mirth. He dipped his honey-blond head near her ear. "Hiding again, little sister?"

He knew her too well.

She shook her head before taking a sip of the overly-sweet beverage. "No, I'm just avoiding—"

"Is that Kingsley?" Gaze as steely and cold as his tone, Giles canted his head to a cluster of guests not more than thirty feet away.

Philomena had thought Bradford attractive across the wide room, but this devilish, rake was garnering moon-eyed sighs and giggles from the younger misses and calculating, seductive glances from the faster, mature set. He hadn't seen her yet, and she wheeled around, presenting her back. The air clamped in her lungs so fiercely, her head spun dizzily, and her glass slipped from her hand. "Oh, dear God."

Her ragged gasp alerted Giles, and he seized her drink, preventing an embarrassing mishap or calling Bradford's attention to her.

Scorn sharpened the planes of his thin face as he scowled at Bradford. Quaffing his remaining punch, Giles then tossed back her ratafia before taking both cups in one hand and maneuvering her into the crowd. His gaze, simmering with sympathy, plucked at her self-control.

"Why don't we take a turn about the terrace, Phil? A bit of fresh air might help steady your nerves and allow you a few moments to compose yourself."

So that you don't make an utter cake of yourself.

She refused to peek over her shoulder, stiffening her spine until the taut muscles between her shoulder blades pinched.

Had the women fluttering their eyelashes and sending coquettish smiles Bradford's way any notion how ridiculous they looked? Scant difference lay between their brazen invitations and those of seasoned, dockside harlots. Not that Philomena blamed them. He'd matured into an arresting figure of a man, while she concealed hideous scars, necessitating a gown far from the first peak of fashion.

Jealousy dowsed with pain nipped her heart. Once upon a time, he had reserved that charming, sensual smile for her alone. Well, she'd convinced her naïve, younger self he had.

"It's just there, through those French windows. You go along, and I'll be right out after I find Lady Middleton's misplaced shawl and put these down or find a servant to take them." Giles nodded in the doors' direction and half-lifted the glasses. "Earlier, I noticed a charming path through the gardens we might stroll."

And exhaust himself further? No. A secluded bench was a far better option.

Dragging her musings from Bradford, flashing his enigmatic smile at the tittering females, Philomena gave a short jerk of her head. "Yes, yes, fresh air and a stroll. An excellent notion."

Escape before the tears she swore she'd stopped shedding for him breached the damn of her resolve and surged down her cheeks. Why did seeing him hurt so awfully after all this time?

She should be over him. Wanted to be over him. Had thought she was until this miserable instant. Joy and anguish at seeing him again wrestled fiercely, each vying for supremacy.

Stupid, fickle heart.

Curling her gloved fingers into fists, and with determination in each step, she deftly navigated through the throng, her focus locked on her refuge—the lantern-lit garden. Perhaps, like a mythical tree nymph, she could disappear into the greeneries for the rest of the evening. Truth be known, no one but Giles would miss her.

Bradford hadn't sent a single letter, not one, the miserable wretch. And neither had he attempted to contact her or Giles after the fire that took Mama's and Papa's lives and nearly hers as well. A blaze that had destroyed their home and that Bradford's fiend of an uncle had started in the sanctuary—accidentally, he claimed, the lying bugger.

Day after day during the months of her convalescence, Philomena had hoped and prayed Bradford would come to see her or at least send word. Her love gave her strength, gave her the will to fight to live, helped her bear the anguish of her healing burns and the horrific loss of her parents and home.

By the time she left her sick-bed, she had relinquished any expectation of hearing from him again. Standing before her aunt's filmy dressing table mirror,

Philomena cringed at the havoc the fire had wreaked on her arms and chest. Yet she possessed a measure of gratitude too, that except for a few minor burns on her shoulders and neck, the rest of her body had been spared. Taking her heart and her youthful love, scarred as viciously as her body, she'd tucked them away, determined never to endure pain that torturous again.

Bradford's shallow promises—that he'd love her until the end of time, that as soon as he was old enough, he'd ask for her hand, that he couldn't wait to marry her, that their difference in stations didn't matter—all lies. He hadn't wanted a maimed wife after the fire, and now that he held a title, he could choose a diamond of the first water for his viscountess.

Bitter knowledge to her injured pride and wounded soul.

"You knew you'd probably see him, Phil." Giles steered her further away from the salivating dames and the man who'd trampled her heart. He pressed her elbow. "It's the talk of London, his arriving in England on the cusp of his uncle's death. At least you were spared his company the better part of the Season. And you've suitors aplenty to choose from. Why, just this evening, Mr. Wrightly asked if he might court you."

"He did?"

How ghastly.

Double her age, the thrice-widowed, rich nabob made no secret he sought a young wife to beget an heir on. Coarse, vulgar, and perpetually reeking of rancid lard and sweat, Mr. Wrightly had finally deduced no lady of consequence would consider his suit, so he'd lowered his standards and now directed his attention to Philomena.

Lucky her. As if she were that desperate. Yet. "Please tell me you said no."

"Of course I didn't." Giles affected an insulted mien. "That's for you to decide, but you must make a decision by this Season's end. We haven't the funds to sponsor another."

Neither would he likely live that long.

A quartet of giggling misses, trailed by plain-faced Lady Victoria Southwark, staring longingly at Bradford, plowed across their path, scurrying toward the row of chairs to which he had escorted his sister. Obvious as fur on a frog what they schemed. Empty-headed chits.

"We've nearly used the whole of what Aunt Alice bequeathed us." Tense lines bracketing his mouth, Giles veered his attention from the women.

He wouldn't even permit himself interest in a woman, and sympathy welled at the unfairness of his plight. What a superb husband and father he would have made.

"I know, Giles, and I am trying. Truly."

Philomena compelled her stiff lips to smile. They'd exhausted their connections as well, and if it hadn't been for imposing upon Aunt Alice's distant relation to the Dowager Marchioness of Middleton, no door in London would have opened to them—the insignificant offspring of a second son and his equally unremarkable wife. "There are still a few weeks left in the Season. All is not yet lost."

Giles accompanied her toward the open French windows, lines of fatigue already deepening around his bleary eyes. "I'm not worried, Phil. You've caught the attention of several eligible men, and with your beauty and wit, I've no doubt you shall have multiple offers."

Bless him for his optimism, but blinded by brotherly love, he exaggerated her potential. At two and twenty, with a very modest dowry and a torso and arms riddled with scars, she wasn't sought after.

Her beaux consisted of an ancient, almost deaf baronet with a mouthful of rotting teeth, a former sea captain who yet retained a cargo hold's peculiar odor, a pimply-faced youth in line for an earldom, whose mother had towed him away by his ear upon finding him declaring himself to Philomena at a musicale last week, a banker so tight in the pocket he'd worn the exact same clothing every time she'd encountered him and was wont to stuff his pockets with food when he thought no one looked, a fourth son, without a farthing to his name and a propensity to ogle every bosom within ten feet, and now—*God bless my remarkable good fortune*—the widower, Mr. Wrightly.

Yes, they made a dandy selection to pick from. Why, Philomena was all aflutter, trying to determine which of the extraordinary gentlemen to set her cap for. However could she possibly choose between them?

But choose she must.

To ease Giles's fretting, she'd given her word she would marry, in spite of not wishing to ever enter that state, and they truly had exhausted most of their meager funds. Despite making economies, they'd only enough money to pay the rent and their expenses through July. To keep them from the poor house, and prevent him from seeking employment, she must wed. He was too weak, and sure as the rich guzzled champagne, acquiring a menial position would mean a speedier end for him.

If any one of her suitors didn't set her stomach to roiling worse than a pitching deck during a tempest, she would've said her vows tomorrow.

Squaring her shoulders, Philomena offered him what she hoped was a brave smile.

What needs done, gets done.

Hopefully, none of her admirers lurked outside, for she'd no wish to encounter them alone. She hadn't curbed her tendency to speak her mind, an attribute not favored by males, and she wasn't in a position to spurn anyone's attentions just yet.

Almost to the exit, she touched his arm. "I'll meet you outside, Giles, as soon as you are able. Who knows, I might stumble upon yet another potential husband upon the terrace."

And Lady Clutterbuck might cease gossiping, and snowflakes won't melt in hell.

Haggard lines creased Giles's eyes, and he gave her a firm nudge. "Miss Kingsley is looking this way. Hurry, Phil, go before she recognizes us."

2

"**M**ake it something quite spectacular, will you? Something scandalous to keep their forked tongues flapping for a good long while." Bradford winked and grinned at his sister and her soon-to-be-husband before spinning on his heel. Allen Wimpleton had just proposed to Olivia, and he wouldn't stay and intrude upon his sister's special moment.

Not exactly proper brotherly advice, Kingsley, especially for a viscount.

He'd never much adhered to, nor much cared for, the *haute ton's* version of propriety. Hadn't he just proven that by escaping outdoors? The dozen or so introductions he had endured, mostly to wide-eyed, blushing misses, had quite put him off, and he'd absconded to the garden a half hour after arriving without dancing once or even greeting Lord and Lady Wimpleton. Quite beyond the pale, even for him.

Bradford mentally shrugged. So what?

After glimpsing a woman reminding him of a lost love, joy and shock had momentarily stunned him before reality cruelly whispered the truth. Blanketed in a cloak of disappointment, he'd sought a few moments alone and come upon his sister and her beau.

Perhaps Wimpleton and Olivia would indulge in a wholly inappropriate kiss in full view of the guests mingling on the terrace. Bradford heartily hoped so. He would if he were them. If a dame or two had a fit of the vapors as result, so much the better. At least this ball would be memorable, and the hullabaloo added a degree of interest to an otherwise wholly predictable, and altogether boring, evening.

Whistling to the strains of a waltz filtering through the open French windows, he strode the curved flagstone footpath deeper into the manicured gardens, lit here and there by lanterns atop wrought iron posts.

The giggles, rustles, and muffled groans emanating from the shrubberies he passed hinted at activities much more outrageous than the sweethearts' *tete-a-tete* he'd just witnessed. Olivia and Allen adored each other, and if they wanted to express their love publicly, so be it. Stuff the *Beau Monde's* pompous posturing and endless hypocritical rules.

A throaty laugh floated from a bush several feet away.

Brow raised, Bradford hustled by the shuddering greenery lest he find himself privy to a rather intimate display.

Awkward, that.

On second thought, perchance a modicum of wisdom ought to be observed regarding engaging in public affection. How those tumbling about in the foliage with the abandon of frisky field mice or amorous squirrels expected their mussed hair or wrinkled and stained clothing to go undetected confounded him. Unless they'd stripped stark naked before coupling.

Bare arses bobbing amongst leaves?

He chuckled softly. Wouldn't that raise a few eyebrows? Probably lecherous ogling, too.

Life was meant to be fun and enjoyed, and by Jove, he fully intended to do just that. Better to have a damned jolly time of it, make the most of every moment—as long as he didn't hurt others as he went about his larks. In any event, his wicked wit and hunger for excitement made it impossible to do otherwise. However, his recently acquired title put a confounded damper on things, a cumbersome yoke of responsibility and duty he'd never expected—nor wanted.

Though now that he bore a title, he still didn't know how many days he might have left on this earth, or what twists or obstacles destiny might hurl his way. His new status gave testament to that. His uncle, the former viscount, and cousins—the heir and the spare— had drowned in a boating accident mere months after Father succumbed to apoplexy, thrusting the viscountcy upon an unenthusiastic Bradford.

Death had brushed her icy fingertips across his soul not so very long ago as well, and though he'd escaped with his life, two of the sugar mill workers had not. Mother had died far too young, too, and Philomena—his sweet Phil—had been on the cusp of womanhood when tragedy struck and stole her from him.

His earlier levity fled.

Twice in less than fifteen minutes, she'd stampeded into his thoughts. Shouldn't he be beyond such melancholy reflections by now? He'd known many women since her death, some astonishingly beautiful, witty, and intelligent, yet his heart remained numb and unengaged.

Quite simply, Philomena had been exquisite—the others, forgettable.

Perchance that was his lot, to love only once.

Blast, but he craved a cheroot, the singular bad habit he'd acquired from his sire. One he'd nearly succeeded in putting aside, after witnessing his father's labored breathing at the end of his life, except for moments such as these, when desperation for the familiar calmative overcame Bradford.

Cursed weakness.

Doubly-cursed memories.

Slowing his pace, he sought a private corner to indulge. If he recalled correctly—he hadn't been to the Wimpleton's in over three years—an almost concealed arbor lay nestled in the far corner of the grounds. Few guests had ventured this far from the mansion, and he welcomed the solitude, finding London much too crowded, confining, and noisy after three years living in the Caribbean.

Blessed wonder neither he nor Olivia had contracted Yellow Fever, or one of the other foul illnesses prevalent in the tropics—precisely why, in addition to opposing slavery, he'd sold the blasted plantation and booked passage to England as soon as they'd laid Father to rest.

A sweet fragrance wafted past.

Honeysuckle.

Warm and subtly erotic, the scent triggered youthful recollections of love lost. Again. Wistfulness he'd not experienced in a long while seized him. He'd have married Philomena had she lived. At six and twenty, he'd yet to find another woman who made him feel even a fraction of what he'd felt for her as a fumbling youth.

Ah, there stood the arbor, at the end of the path where the glow of two lanterns penetrated the shadows. Bradford quickened his pace, canvassing the area.

Alone.

Perfect, he'd take a puff or two, just enough to satisfy his craving, and then return to the ball. A ravishing brunette had caught his eye earlier. Even after all these years, he couldn't bring himself to direct his attentions to fair-haired women. It seemed a betrayal of Philomena's memory. If he could finagle an introduction, he was of a mind to ask the dark-haired beauty to save a dance for him. It shouldn't be at all difficult to arrange. He was prime stock on the Marriage Mart these days.

As Mr. Kingsley, he'd been an agreeable companion, comfortable in the pocket, a nice fellow to have about. Suitable, but not hotly pursued. As Viscount Kingsley, however, he could scarcely make a public appearance without forward Mamas thrusting their eligible daughters in his path. However, he'd no intention of acquiring a viscountess just yet. Adjusting to his new position, as well as acclimating to England again, was quite enough to take on at once. He wasn't a damned martyr, for God's sake. He'd have to be addled to take on a bride at present.

He felt rather like one of the savory dishes his hostess had laid out for supper. Not at all pleasant to be eyed like a tasty morsel, or lusted after by ladies of the *ton* more brazen than a Covent Garden strumpet.

Earlier, a seductive-eyed, full-bosomed peeress had given him a lecherous wink and licked her full lower lip suggestively. Her bold invitation left him cold. Or, perhaps her unfortunate eyebrows, melding into a single furry line across her forehead that wriggled and writhed when she spoke had prompted his escape to the gardens where he'd discovered Allen and Olivia.

He ought to have been outraged upon interrupting their tryst, but relief that they'd quickly made amends had spurred genuine happiness for them. At least one Kingsley would have a youthful promise fulfilled. His hopes for love had died with Philomena.

At the bower's entrance, a movement overhead caught Bradford's attention. He gave a crooked smile as several shooting stars streaked across the midnight-blue sky. Closing his eyes, he wished Olivia and Allen a lifetime of happiness.

And lots of babies. He quite looked forward to being an outrageous uncle.

Sentimental sot.

He cracked an eye open. Two more flashes whooshed above, their feathery tails leaving a reminder of the universe's vastness and his insignificance.

Such an opportunity shouldn't be wasted, even if it was superstitious drivel.

Wasn't every day the sky lit up like fireworks over Vauxhall Gardens. His eyelids drifted shut once more.

I want to find the passion true love promises again—

"—to experience true love's kiss," a beguiling feminine voice whispered.

His eye popped open.

A woman surveyed the heavens, the moon illuminating her upturned face and flaxen hair as she rested one shoulder against the other entrance's post. In her white gown, a wide, whitish ribbon encircling her curls, and her features faintly blurry in the half light, she appeared ethereal. Angelic.

"You made a wish too." Bradford stepped forward.

Giving a startled squeak, she whirled to face him and tripped on something—a root or uneven stone, perhaps. Unbalanced, she flailed her arms, dropping her fan.

He sprang forward and caught the tempting armful around her trim back. Generous breasts pressed his chest, leaving two molten spots, and her fragrant hair teased his nose. Inhaling the flowery essence blending with the honeysuckle-laden air, he tightened his embrace. She fit into the hollow of his arms as snugly as a hand fits a custom-made glove, her plentiful curves promising passion.

Who was she?

"Good God, are you insane?" She scrambled free of his embrace then gave his chest a forceful shove. "You scared the stuffing out of me and ten years off my life, you ill-mannered lout. You might damn-well warn someone before you prowl up behind them unawares."

Though he couldn't see her features clearly, he didn't doubt the sharp-tongued angel glowered at him as she bent to retrieve her fan.

"What are you doing gadding about out here alone?" She jabbed the accessory toward the path. "Shouldn't you be inside dancing, or seducing, or doing whatever handsome, privileged men do at these affairs?"

What was *she* doing lurking in the bower alone?

"How do you know I'm handsome? I could be a pock-scarred, toothless troll." He couldn't identify her in the shadowy enclosure. Had they been introduced tonight? "It's too dark to make out my features. I know, because I'm doing my utmost to see your face. If it's anything like your voice, I can expect utter loveliness."

"Of all the flowery hogwash—" She poked her head out the entrance, her champagne-colored hair shiny in the lantern light, and after looking both ways, she retreated deep into the bower.

Was she expecting someone? Not unusual. Many lovers took advantage of gatherings to indulge in an assignation. Disappointment that she waited for someone prodded him, nonetheless.

"I beg your pardon," she said. "That was unpardonably rude."

Transparent, honest, and quick to apologize. How refreshing. Perhaps she truly was an angel.

"I've never been able to bridle my waspish tongue, I'm afraid." Her husky, self-conscious laugh had him imagining all sorts of things she might do with her tongue.

Bradford edged nearer. Something niggled in the back of his mind. They'd met before. He'd bet on it. Probably before Father had hied him and Olivia off to the sweltering, disease-riddled ends of the earth.

Three years wasted on a doddering old fool's pursuit.

Ah, well. Naught could be done to alter the past. He much preferred the present and the intriguing sprite hovering in the arbor. He typically avoided blondes, but this woman with her light hair drew him. "No apology necessary. I confess, I was so disconcerted by your wish mirroring mine, I didn't think to alert you to my presence."

"You did give me a tremendous start." Releasing a musical laugh, she flipped her fan open and waved it before her, not coyly but fervently, as if overheated. "I confess. I'm mortified you overheard my wish. You must think me a ninny, talking to myself."

He was forgiven. Just like that. No pouting or fussing. Definitely an angelic being.

"Not a bit of it." After all, his wish had been as silly. "I dare say, we are at our most honest when we speak to ourselves, are we not?"

"Hmm, I suppose."

In the nebulous lighting, he couldn't read her expression.

She wore an unusual gown. Not the typical capped sleeve with a wide expanse of bosom exposed. Her sleeves fastened tightly around her wrists, and the neckline covered her collarbone.

Perhaps she was bent on creating a new fashion or didn't give a whit about current trends. Or, unlike a number of ladies present at the ball, wearing dampened gowns and bodices that all but exposed their nipples, she claimed exceptional modesty.

In any event, the gown overlaid with some sort of golden overskirt shimmered in the filtered light and clung to her form, reaffirming what he'd discovered when he'd held her in his arms. She possessed a goddess's supple figure; just the sort of woman he favored in his bed.

Digging into his memory's bowels, he couldn't produce a whit of recollection regarding where he'd met this treasure or what her name might be. Having spent the last years abroad, tending a declining sugar plantation—a loathsome task since he abhorred slavery—while Olivia nursed their sickly father, Bradford, a self-confessed, dismally poor correspondent, had lost contact with his school chums and those previously in the Kingsleys' social circle.

"I know it's devilishly boorish of me, and utterly improper, but please allow me to introduce myself, though I feel certain we've met before."

"I know who you are, Viscount." Snapping her fan closed, she peered out the entrance again, the lanterns' light bathing her face. She gave him a sideways look. Not coyness exactly, more guarded uncertainty, and she definitely expected someone. "All of London is abuzz about the return of the Kingsleys and your good fortune in acquiring a title and wealth."

"Not sure my uncle and cousins would see it that way as they all drowned." He swatted distractedly at a tiny insect flitting about his head. Nothing compared to the hordes of blood-sucking, bird-sized tropical mosquitoes.

"You have my condolences." Her stiffly offered commiserations rang falsely.

Curious.

"I'm convinced my uncle would have eaten his Wellingtons with his few remaining teeth, rather than entertain the notion I would ever inherit the viscountcy." Bradford had never entertained the idea either. "The entailment gave him no choice, however."

Pity, that.

Herbert Kingsley had been an unethical, avaricious curmudgeon obsessed with peerage purity and wholly contemptuous of commoners. He barely tolerated peers' kin, deeming all but those holding the highest ranking beneath his touch.

Considering that even in his prime, the miserly chap couldn't boast more than four inches beyond five feet tall, and he'd shrunk to a wizened shell of a man by the time he met his fate amongst the fishes, the notion that anyone was beneath him tickled Bradford's irregular sense of humor.

"You weren't close to your uncle? I'd heard—" She cocked her head, and a moonbeam illuminated the lower portion of her face, revealing a pert chin and Cupid's bow lips, the lower clamped between her small, white teeth.

What color were her eyes? Blue as was typical of many blondes? And what did she know of his uncle? For more than half a decade, Herbert had sequestered himself at Bromham Hall, and except for infrequent and unsolicited encounters with his heir, Horace, a cocksure weakling of dubious moral character, Bradford seldom had news of the sot his father had once called brother.

"He didn't hold you in his confidence? I thought the Kingsleys an intimate, closed-mouth family, wary of outsiders." The angel cast a harried glance to the entrance before edging nearer to Bradford.

Had he interrupted a lover's assignation? Annoyance jabbed at Bradford's jealousy, doing its utmost to garner a reaction from him. He quashed the impulse. What she did in secluded, moonlit vestibules wasn't his concern.

Then why did it trouble him so much?

"Indeed, not. I hadn't spoken to him since ..." Since the fire that stole Philomena ... No. He wasn't trudging down that lengthy and ghoulish trail. He scratched his jaw just below his ear. "Well, in very long while. You might say we were at permanent odds. What had you heard?"

She stood before him now, so close he could touch her—brush her silky cheek with his thumb or cheek. The graceful curve of her mouth—lips molded for kissing—snared his attention. Her enticing perfume enveloped him once more, demanding he recall where he'd seen—*and smelled?*—her before.

Blast and damn, why couldn't he remember?

"At odds?" She peered up at him, her gaze unpretentious. "Why?"

Did confusion dance across her features? The pale light filtering through the lattice might have caused the illusion.

He brushed her jaw, the flesh warm and silky, with his knuckles. "You oughtn't to be out here alone. What if an unscrupulous chap came upon you?"

"How do I know you aren't just such a man?" She didn't pull away, though her breaths came quick and shallow, and she swallowed before wetting her lips. Not the reaction of a woman meeting her lover. "Even now, you might harbor dishonorable designs."

His pulse leaped. Oh, he had an idea or two, but he wouldn't call the musings dishonorable, more along the order of improper, but absolutely delicious, sensual imaginings. Not altogether wise, contemplating kissing a nameless woman in an obscure arbor housed in the gardens of his soon-to-be-brother-in-law.

The moisture glistening on her plump and pink lower lip, enticed temptingly.

But, then again, who was he to turn down such an unexpected and precious gem? He was about to see one of the fantasies of a moment ago realized.

Bradford lowered his head a couple of inches, and her sooty eyelashes swooped downward, fanning her cheeks. Hovering over her parted lips, her breath sweet and slightly fruity as if she'd eaten berries, he booted caution aside.

What could one kiss hurt? He had no intention of taking the moment as far as those in the bushes outside. Perhaps if he kissed her, he would finally recall how he knew her.

No, fool. If you'd ever kissed this woman before, you'd not have forgotten.

True. This woman would leave her mark on a man's soul. Savoring the moment, he trailed his tongue along the seam of her lips, wanting her to experience the same enchantment encompassing him. How easily he could become snared in this temptress's grasp. He nipped the corner of her mouth.

She gasped and gripped his forearms, swaying slightly before relaxing into his chest and offering her parted lips.

Gathering her into his arms, he pressed his mouth to hers. Lust exploded, flooding through his veins and roaring in his ears. Tendrils of want wended around his senses, and he pulled her closer, deepening their kiss and cupping her lush buttocks.

"Pray tell, what the hell do you think you are doing mauling my sister, Kingsley?"

3

For the second time in ten minutes, Philomena gave a startled yelp and lost her balance—only this time, mortification licked her cheeks, and the muscled arms already encircling her kept her steady. Averting her gaze, she slipped from Bradford's embrace. Putting a respectable distance between them, she retreated to the bower's corner where she could observe her brother and the man she had once loved without revealing her flustered state.

Or before Bradford finally recognized her.

She unfurled her fan open to cool the blast of warmth suffusing her.

What did it matter if he discovered her identity? He would know soon enough. It changed nothing, and she certainly wasn't going to make a scene about the kiss. Absurd, this hurt constricting her chest because he still hadn't realized who she was.

He had truly forgotten her.

She had known him the instant he entered the Wimpleton's gilded ballroom. But then, to be fair, a hundred blazing candles lit the room, and here, only silvery moonbeams filtered through the rose-covered arbor. Nonetheless, she would have recognized him anywhere. The way he moved, the timbre of his voice, the angle of his head, his animal grace ... his scent.

His essence had long ago been etched into her memory—her soul—and could no more be erased or obliterated than she could change her eye color. In her youthful naiveté, she'd thought the same true of him, but he *had* forgotten her, and the knowledge sent a fresh surge of betrayal to her heart.

In the bower's seclusion, he'd taken her in his arms, but he had also given her the opportunity to resist, to pull away, and she hadn't. She'd lifted her mouth in anticipation, wanting the kiss she'd been denied as a constantly chaperoned miss during his visits.

Hadn't she wished for that very thing a mere moment before?

No, she'd wished for *true* love's kiss, and Bradford had proven he didn't love her.

Utterly foolish, however, indulging in an actual kiss. It only served as reminder of that which she would never have. Besides, Giles had been most clear he regarded his former friend as his greatest foe, and her presence at the ball was for one purpose only.

To snare a husband as swiftly as possible—God forgive her—and Bradford was beyond her reach now.

Nevertheless, she wouldn't regret her impulsive action. When he'd slipped into the arbor, time propelled her back seven years, to the innocent girl, too young and protected to do more than hold hands and make secret, fervent vows of undying love. A shallow, youthful love—at least on his part—incapable of enduring hardship and separation.

Her wish, cast upon a series of stars pelting across the heavens, had been to experience true love's kiss before she surrendered herself to a match of convenience and bore the fumbling and groping of a husband whose touch she only tolerated, or worse, repulsed her.

A delicate shudder skittered across her shoulders.

How shall I bear it?

Giles.

She would do it for him, because he'd sacrificed so much for her.

Risking his life, he'd saved her that terrifying night, pulling her from her bed and carrying her from the inferno as their home disintegrated around them. He'd sought out their peculiar, reclusive aunt with her healing gift and retained the best physician he could afford to tend to Philomena's burns. With no other options for immediate employment, he'd enlisted, sending the majority of his paltry wages home to pay for her medical fees.

Neither she nor her brother had suspected that Aunt Alice had secreted the monies away, along with the dotty woman's life-savings, and when their childless aunt died six months ago, she'd left them a tidy sum. Not enough to live on for a lengthy period, but enough, if they were frugal, to provide Philomena the Season Giles insisted upon.

She hadn't wanted to spend their funds on something so frivolous, but he'd quietly confessed that the physician had said his heart grew weaker, and Giles had but months to live. The now familiar pain of losing him blossomed in her chest.

Her brother's courage and selflessness mustn't be for naught, and if her finding a husband brought him peace of mind and extended his life a single day, she would willingly make the sacrifice.

She'd all but given up on him joining her in the garden, he had taken so long. His happening along as she clung to Bradford, savoring his firm lips upon hers, was pure coincidence—or perhaps, it had been providential, because she wasn't positive she would have been able to stop him if he'd wanted more than an ardent kiss.

No, she wasn't sure *she* would have been able to stop. Her girlish daydreams and fantasies fell short of the mark of his devastating, glorious kiss, and once she'd tasted his mouth, coherent thought had fled swifter than a startled bird to wing.

"Well, Kingsley?" Chest heaving and struggling

for breath, Giles shuffled farther into the enclosure. "What say you?"

Had he been running, fearful for Philomena's safety when she wasn't on the veranda as agreed? Dash it all. She oughtn't to have ventured this far, but Mr. Wrightly had appeared, likely in search of her so he could present his address, and to avoid him, she'd fled into the garden's protection. She wasn't ready to refuse him just yet, nor could she force herself to accept him either.

A pleasant twinkle in his eye, Bradford inclined his head, not the least nonplussed. "I humbly beg your pardon. I was overtaken with the magic of the moonlight and the beauty of the woman I found staring at the same shooting stars as I."

"Save your flowery poppycock for someone who appreciates such claptrap." Giles seized a nearby post, and Philomena bit her lip to keep from crying out.

He detested others knowing how weak he became when he exerted himself. He would especially not want Bradford to know. They'd been the best of chums before the fire, swimming, hunting, and riding together whenever Bradford's family came down to the country to visit the viscount.

She crossed to Giles's side. Slipping her arm through his, she winced at the tremors shaking his frail frame.

"Extremely poor judgement on my part, brother dear. Let's go home, shall we? I'm quite done in."

"I fear you have me at a disadvantage." Even in the alcove's dimness, Bradford's teeth flashed brightly. "You know who I am, but I haven't the same privilege."

Giles's breath left him in a long, shuddery hiss, his eyes gone dark and cold as a wintry forest at midnight. When he spoke, the icy disdain in his voice raised the hairs on her nape. "You mean to tell me you don't know who you kissed just now? Who you've so carelessly compromised?"

"Surely a single, chaste kiss doesn't qualify?" Philomena didn't like the turn the conversation had taken, and although she hadn't any experience with kissing, she was positive the tongue tangling, explosion of sensation she'd just experienced had been a far cry from chaste. She tugged at her brother's arm. "Come, let's take our leave. No one but we three need ever know of my foolishness."

That she'd yielded to temptation, too sweet to resist, at the expense of guarding her heart and reputation. *Fool.*

"There was more than innocent kissing going on." Giles jerked his chin toward Bradford. "I saw Kingsley pawing you."

Whether anger or difficulty drawing his breath caused Giles's husky voice, Philomena couldn't determine, but her alarm spiraled. He mustn't become agitated. It stressed his heart too much. "The fault is not entirely his. I shouldn't have been out here alone, and should have returned to the house at once when he entered the bower."

And I kissed him too.

She couldn't bring herself to confess that to Giles. He'd done everything a loving brother could to help her heal as well as forget Bradford's betrayal and abandonment, and she'd cast caution and good sense aside with the ease of a laundress tossing out dirty wash water.

Bradford shook his head, his keen gaze fluctuating between her and Giles. "I confess, I don't, but from your reaction, I fear I should. I thought I should as well, but I've been away from England these three years past, and have never been adept at remembering names."

"Have we changed so very much?" Pulling himself upright, a skeletal shell of the virile man he'd once been, Giles gave a short, harsh laugh.

Yes, he had.

He jerked his head toward Bradford. "Phil, he doesn't even remember us. *You*. The cawker just meant to take advantage of a woman he found alone."

"It wasn't like that at all. Please, you mustn't upset yourself." Philomena yanked on his thin arm. "Let me take you home. I'll prepare a hot toddy to help you sleep, Giles, and—"

"Giles?" Bradford went rigid, and then took a half-step forward before halting abruptly. He shook his head as if dazed, and even in the shadowy light, his probing gaze raked her. "Phil? Philomena Pomfrett?

No, it's not possible. You're dead."

Raw pain and stunned disbelief radiated from his eyes, and his confused expression gave him a helpless, boyish appearance. He shook his head and scraped a hand through his hair, more vulnerable than Philomena had ever seen him.

"Dead? You imbecile, does she look dead?" After shaking off Philomena's restraining hand, Giles stomped the few feet to Bradford. Giles's unreserved wrath spewed forth like a river breaching a dyke, and his face contorted into a snarl as he jabbed Bradford in the chest. "She did almost die and has the scars to prove the hell she endured. Made worse because the man she adored abandoned her."

"I'd been told you died in the fire." His face folding into distraught lines, Bradford held out one hand in entreaty. "Please, you must believe me. I didn't know."

Her breath snagged as compassion welled within her chest. Had he suffered too?

"It doesn't matter. It's in the past. Water over a dam cannot be retrieved." Far too late for recriminations, at this juncture. She touched Giles's forearm, reluctant to reveal that he ailed, but anxious to calm him. Muted voices and a dove's sleepy coo trickled into the garden nook along with a violin's faint strains. "We risk someone coming upon us and overhearing, and that would ruin everything. My suitors mustn't know of this indiscretion."

"Suitors?" Surprise registered on Bradford's face before his features closed. "You've more than one?"

Why so astonished? She wasn't altogether repulsive to gaze upon; at least not clothed. He needn't know her beaux bordered on the dregs of humanity. Piqued, she arched a brow. "Indeed, several as a matter of fact."

Unless her indiscretion became known.

Dear Lord, she'd be ruined. Just like that. All because of the irresistible temptation of true love's kiss. And then what would she and Giles do?

Stupid, rash girl.

Unyielding, his breathing shallow and rapid, Giles glowered at Bradford and flexed his hand as if he wanted to pummel him. He mustn't become more agitated.

"Giles, please. Your heart." She pressed her fingertips together, her heart racing with apprehension.

He would have none of it, however. "Let me guess. Your ruddy uncle told you she died, didn't he, Kingsley? Why am I not surprised? Did it ever occur to you that the manipulative old bugger lied? He reviled us from the moment the bishop appointed Father vicar. Most especially, the cur objected to you spending time with a family he held in such low regard. Did you even attempt to find me, to learn the truth, to see how I fared? After all, you thought I'd lost my entire family and my home."

Philomena flinched as if slapped, an ache burgeoning in her chest. She'd never considered the depth of Giles's hurt and anger, that his dearest friend had never sent his condolences or tried to see him. Absorbed in her physical and emotional pain, she'd been oblivious to his misery, and dear Giles wouldn't burden her with his suffering.

How selfish could she have been?

A cloud drifted across the moon, plunging the arbor into darkness, and her earlier joy along with it.

"My friend, please accept my deepest, most heart-felt apologies, but I thought you dead as well." Closing his eyes for a moment, Bradford rubbed his right temple.

Even in the dim light, she could see the strain pinching his mouth, and she yearned to smooth the tension away with her lips.

"I was beside myself when I heard the news," he said, "and by the time I could bear coming down to Bromhamshire, weeks later, nothing remained of the vicarage and church except the garden wall and the charred bell tower. My uncle claimed all had perished in the fire. In all these years, I haven't returned. Not once."

"Am I supposed to feel sympathy for you?" Giles attempted a laugh, which ended on a wheezing cough. Something was wrong. His breathing rattled and rasped with each labored breath.

"No, but I want you to know I mourned mightily." He sought Philomena's eyes for a brief moment, and she couldn't help but feel he meant the words for her, almost as a request for forgiveness.

Her earlier anger at his callousness faded, replaced by searing regret. They would have been happy together, and now, that bliss was lost to her. He would find some exquisite, unmarred bit of loveliness to wed, and she would settle on whichever man she could most stomach for the rest of her life.

"Perhaps some sixth sense alerted me, and that's why Philomena enchanted me when I saw her just now." He flicked a hand in her direction, though his attention never faltered from Giles.

"My sister is not some fast wench you can dally with." Hand shaking, Giles stripped off a glove then whacked Bradford's face, the slap echoing in the enclosure. "I demand satisfaction."

"Giles, no!" This was a damned fine turn of events. All because she hadn't the backbone to stand up to Mr. Wrightly.

Bradford cupped his cheek. "The devil you do. Are you dicked in the knob? You can barely stand upright."

Philomena pushed her way between the men and pursed her mouth. "You're being utterly absurd.

Please, let's leave, before this situation becomes any more ludicrous."

"It's my responsibility to protect you, Philomena. I may not have long left on this Earth, and I may be as weak as a suckling runt, but by God, I shall see you properly married and set up in your own home before I cock up my toes."

Her eyes misted. He championed her, even sick as a cushion.

Giles swayed and stumbled forward, bumping into the arbor and sending a shower of leaves and petals cascading down upon them.

"Giles!" Something was definitely wrong.

Was there a physician in attendance? Perhaps their hosts could recommend one to her. He needed immediate attention.

"What's this?" Bradford swiftly steadied him. "Are you ill, Pomfrett?"

Giles yanked free and laughed, the rasping bitter and hollow. "No. I'm not ill. I'm dying."

Stunned silence reigned for a pregnant moment.

"My God, you cannot be. You're only ... what?

Seven and twenty?" Forehead puckered, Bradford sent Philomena a beseeching glance. "Consumption?"

Sagging against the lattice, Giles half-closed his eyes. "No. Scarlet Fever. Untreated. Damaged heart. I won't see another Christmastide."

"I'm truly saddened beyond words." Neck bent, Bradford inhaled a hefty breath and rubbed his nape as if overcome with emotion. "Are you sure? I could arrange to have another physician examine you, if you would allow it."

"Won't change anything," Giles said with a rueful slant of his mouth. "I'm as good as gone."

Philomena stifled her agonized protest at his declaration and turned her head away to swipe at the confounded tears that insisted on seeping from her eyes despite her best efforts. "Enough of this wretched talk. I won't hear it. We're going home. Now. And I'm sending for a physician, no matter what you say, Giles."

Surely someone with the manor could recommend a competent fellow whose fees she might afford.

Slouching further into the brace's support, he shut

his eyes and shook his head. "No. Either Kingsley meets me on the field or ..."

Thank God, he had another option besides a confounded duel. Relief weakened her knees, but she managed a tremulous smile. "Or what?"

He slowly opened his eyes, and the bleak despair warring with desperation sliced straight to her soul. "Or he marries you. It's his choice which he does on the morrow."

4

Bradford snapped his head up, his jaw drooping. He didn't see that coming, and he should have. "The devil I shall. Your illness has you talking nonsense, Pomfrett. I'm in agreement with Philomena—"

A bolder moonbeam lit Philomena's stunned countenance, and she hastily averted her face.

"She's Miss Pomfrett to you." Pomfrett pulled his spine straight and faced him, although he swayed like a tree during a storm's onslaught.

Bradford couldn't help but admire Pomfrett's devotion to his sister, though somewhat misplaced. Demanding satisfaction or marriage ... Over a kiss. An eager, willing kiss, at that.

It wasn't as if he'd been caught with his hand up

her skirt. Typical *tonnish* overreaction, except Pomfrett hadn't been raised amongst the upper ten thousand, and Bradford had never known him to be the dramatic sort. Guilt stabbed him. If Wimpleton hadn't already offered Olivia marriage, Bradford would have demanded he do right by his sister too.

That made him the worst sort of hypocrite.

"I'll have my satisfaction. You will—" Shaking a finger at him, Pomfrett suddenly choked on a gasp then clawed at his chest.

"Oh, my God, no!" Philomena lurched forward, trying to catch her brother as he slumped. "What's wrong?"

The terror in her voice congealed Bradford's blood. Pomfrett spoke truthfully; he wasn't long for this world.

Bradford reached him first, managing to prevent her brother from plowing into the pavers. Illness had ravaged his sparse frame, and Pomfrett weighed little more than a woman.

"Philomena, hurry to the house and request Wimpleton send for a physician."

"No, no." Pomfrett shook his head. "I just need to sit. I know better than to become overwrought." He tapped his chest feebly. "The ol' ticker doesn't like it. Blood doesn't flow like it ought."

Philomena came round to Pomfrett's other side and, after wrapping her arm about his waist, helped Bradford lead her brother to the bench at the rear of the enclosure. Bradford might have carried him to the house but feared wounding Pomfrett's pride.

Once he'd taken a seat, Philomena set to loosening her brother's neckcloth. Bent over him, she brushed his pale hair off his forehead and presented Bradford a delightful view of her rounded backside.

"Please let Bradford send for a doctor. I would feel ever so much better."

Did she realize she'd addressed him by his given name? He'd never thought to hear his name on her pretty lips again, and pleasure coiled around his ribs.

God, he'd missed her musical voice, the graceful length of her creamy neck, the way she wrinkled her nose and cocked her head when deep in thought—her sultry laugh which could cause the most staid person to smile.

"There's nothing to be done, Phil. I shall be fine. Just give me a few minutes." Pomfrett patted her cheek before resting his head against the arbor's wall. "The leech would want to bleed me in any event, and I'm not forfeiting another drop of blood to cure my ill humors. Leaves me nauseated and weak every time."

Gracefully sinking onto the seat beside him, she took his hand. "I agree. Senseless practice, but perhaps he can prescribe something to calm you and help you sleep."

"Laudanum? I think not. Leaves me wooly-headed, and I cannot abide the bittersweet odor. Gags me, it does." Pomfrett grunted or cleared his throat. Hard to tell which. "I'd rather have a glass of fine Scotch."

Something he likely hadn't indulged in for a very long while. Bradford made a mental note to ask Wimpleton where he might procure a bottle or two of top-notch whisky.

Standing to the side, Bradford slanted his head. That Philomena and her brother held one another in the deepest affection was clear. What would he do if he were dying and Olivia had no means of support, no family to rely on? Wouldn't he be just as frantic to see her provided for before he passed?

At two and twenty, some dolts might consider Philomena past her prime, on the shelf even, and Pomfrett had said she bore scars from the fire, hence her unique gown. If known, that made her an undesirable to most of the shallow coves seeking wives, further reducing her chance of acquiring a respectable match.

Just how badly had she been burned?

His stomach clenched into a gnarled mass that threatened to burst. The pain she'd borne ... God, it didn't bear pondering. The thought left a sour taste in his mouth and a leaden lump in his throat. That his Phil should be reduced to accepting the hand of someone unworthy of her made him gnash his teeth.

Life proved savage to a woman without means or protection. London's East End teemed with harlots, many from respectable backgrounds, who had been left with no recourse to avoid starvation other than to lift their skirts for coin. Such a life guaranteed disease and an early death.

Philomena would not suffer such a fate.

Tilting his head skyward, he drew in a long breath and searched the fragments of firmament visible between the arbor and greenery. Stars flashed and winked a millennium away, but none careened across the expanse.

The Almighty wasn't doling out any more wishes tonight.

"So, what's it to be, Kingsley? Pistols or the parson's mousetrap?"

The air left his lungs in a whoosh, Pomfrett's feeble rasp and failed attempt at humor unceremoniously plummeting Bradford back to Earth.

Philomena made an impolite noise, somewhere between a snort and growl, and plunked her hands on her hips.

Bradford hid a grin.

"Do stop, Giles! He shan't do either. Leave off with that silliness, or I shall become quite cross with you." Worry rather than censure tinged her words. Her eyebrows swooping upward, she sent Bradford an apologetic smile.

Such an expressive face. She'd always been so readable, her candid, wide-eyed gaze giving away her every thought. And outspoken too. She didn't mince words, didn't dance around pretext or use coy innuendoes. If she thought something, she usually said it.

"This once, I'll bear your displeasure, my dear." His mouth compressed into a stern line, Pomfrett stared at Bradford expectantly. "Well, what shall it be?"

No force in heaven or hell could compel Bradford to meet the dying man on the field of honor, especially not over a single kiss, and Pomfrett damn well knew it.

Nevertheless, what a way to re-enter Polite Society. Scarcely a week back in England and Bradford had been challenged to duel, not that he gave a ballock what others might make of it. An hour ago, he might have cared a mite for Olivia's sake, but she was neatly betrothed now, so ... Cock a snook at them all.

Marriage hadn't crossed his mind either, at least not for a good while, though his pesky title now obligated him to find a wife and beget an heir someday. He rubbed the bridge of his nose. What he wouldn't give for a cheroot and a swallow—a bottle—of brandy.

Meshing his lips, he scuffed his shoe across the flagstone, the blood rushing in his ears.

Only one thing to do, fiend seize it, and he would only consider it because Philomena was the woman. She made the sacrifice worthwhile. He plowed his fingers through his hair and tried not to sneer the word, for her sake.

"Marriage."

"I beg your pardon? Have you taken leave of your senses?" Philomena gasped and lurched to her feet, outrage fairly billowing from her in tense waves. She flapped her hand back and forth, gesturing between them. "We cannot marry. Most ridiculous thing I ever heard." She touched her eyebrow and squinted her eyes as if her head hurt. "Completely preposterous," she muttered, glaring at him. "I shall not marry you."

Arms folded, Bradford crooked one side of his mouth upward, not the least surprised by her vehement denial though, her fervency did rather bite. "See there, Pomfrett. She won't have me. That's the end of it, then."

Her refusal rubbed the wrong way—chafed his arse, truth to tell—even if Bradford hadn't been thrilled about a forced union. Philomena had always been his choice for a wife, and now that she'd miraculously risen from the dead, the idea held merit. Great appeal, in truth.

Just not at this precise moment or under these circumstances.

Hell, who did he think he fooled?

He'd marry her tonight if she'd have him.

Bloody good thing his uncle already lay rotting, or Bradford would have choked the life from the worthless cull for lying about her death. And Pomfrett's. The manipulating cur had suspected Bradford intended to offer for her, and even though he was only fourth in line for the title, wanted to ensure a lowly vicar's daughter didn't become Viscountess Kingsley. Why else would he have gone to such extremes to keep the truth from him?

Any sympathy Bradford had entertained about his uncle's drowning fled on the cool breeze wafting into the enclosure.

Pomfrett pressed a hand to his forehead. "Phil, though I'm not keen on the idea of you marrying this bounder, you must admit, he's far superior to the others."

Indeed? How many others?

"And how is coercing him into marrying me better exactly?" She flung Bradford a brusque look.

Offering a puny grin, Pomfrett quipped, "He has all his teeth, and he smells rather nice."

Her determined chin jutted up as she leveled him a withering look. "The Season is not yet over. I may still attract the attention of someone else."

"Who can offer you a title, a fortune, and who you already know?" Bradford shook his head. They'd gotten on well before, and the misunderstanding about her death aside, he saw no reason they shouldn't again. "I don't think so. Phil, be sensible."

"I am being sensible. I am not the naïve young girl I once was, and a title and fortune hold no allure for me. As for knowing you, youthful infatuation does not make a solid basis for a successful marriage, and I'd be a gullible fool for thinking otherwise." She flicked a bit of something off her skirt. "The adults we've become know nothing of the other."

Pomfrett valiantly pulled himself upright and faced her. "It would ease my mind greatly if you married Kingsley, and I would be spared further outings. They do rather test my stamina, and I'm finding it increasingly difficult to manage. And Phil, the doctor advised rest, even taking the waters at Bath. That I cannot do until I see you wed."

To admit to his weakness must have come at a tremendous cost to Pomfrett's pride.

"I know, Giles," Philomena whispered, folding her hands in her lap and tucking her chin to her chest, her voice thickened by tears. "I'm sorry to be a burden."

Pomfrett gathered her into his arms and kissed her temple. "Stuff and nonsense. I never said you were a burden. I know you had deep feelings for Kingsley at one time, and that cannot be said of any of your others suitors. I've more of a desire to see you happy long after I'm gone then marched down the aisle with someone you can never care for."

"I know you only have my best interests at heart." Acute consternation turned her pretty mouth down, and she fiddled with her fan's handle. Shoulders slumping, she released a long-suffering sigh. "I just wasn't prepared to wed so unexpectedly."

Bradford certainly understood that. Since learning that she lived a few moments ago, his thoughts clanged around his skull, helter-skelter, making it deuced impossible to form a coherent thought.

Married.

He gave a sardonic shake of his head. He'd been worried about Olivia's reception this evening and what would happen when she encountered Wimpleton again. Egads, now it seemed he, too, was destined to marry his first love, only unlike Olivia and Wimpleton's joyous match, his bride might choose him as the least undesirable of her suitors.

Rather humbling.

Bradford eased to the entrance, not only to give them privacy, but to check on the prattle growing ever louder. Others approached, and he'd rather have this conversation kept amongst the Pomfretts and himself.

He folded his arms and crossed his ankles, leaning a shoulder against a supporting brace. Of its own accord, his gaze trailed to Philomena before he drew it back to rest on the signet ring circling his little finger. He couldn't see the Kingsley crest or motto engraved there, but he'd heard it his entire life.

Misericordia et Fortitudo. Compassion and courage.

Philomena possessed both in abundance. He could ask for no finer viscountess, and even if her dress covered a myriad of unsightly scars, she was his choice.

"I propose we wait three weeks to wed. Olivia and I are currently staying with our aunt, the Duchess of Daventry, as my uncle let the Mayfair house." *Anything to gain a farthing or two.* "I need time to find us accommodations, since I've never been partial to the place and have no interest in living there. Three weeks allows time to have the banns read, and also eliminates gossip fodder."

"I suppose that's more acceptable, and," Philomena extracted a kerchief from her bodice, "it's not quite so rushed." She dabbed at her eyes. Not ecstatic at the notion, by any means.

"No." Pomfrett shook his head. "It is not acceptable."

"But, Giles ..." She slowly lowered her hand, confusion and chagrin warring in her eyes.

He waved her off with a curt flip of his wrist. "I must insist you wed Philomena tomorrow by special license. If I die within the next three weeks—" A strangled cry escaped Philomena, and Pomfrett patted her knee before continuing. "Mourning protocol would require her to wait at least a year to wed. That I cannot—shall not—allow. She has no funds to live on and nowhere to go."

Her cheeks dashed scarlet, she majestically lifted her head. "That's none of his lordship's affair. I should manage somehow."

Ah, here came the formality. He'd been Bradford till now.

"How, pray tell?" Frustration and desperation hardened Pomfrett's voice. "I've thought this through, from every possible position. If I die before you are wed, you are destitute, Phil." He clasped her hands in both of his. "You know what that could mean. I won't have it, I tell you."

His voice broke on the last word.

Tears tracked down her high cheekbones, and it was all Bradford could do not to gather her in his arms and promise her anything she desired to dry her eyes and bring a smile to her beautiful face once more.

To allow Philomena and Pomfrett time to marshal their composure, Bradford dipped his head on the pretense of sniffing a fully-bloomed peach rose. He inhaled too deeply and sneezed.

"Even if I can procure an appointment with the Archbishop of Canterbury on the morrow, I still need time to find lodgings for us." One suitable for his exquisite bride, though Aunt Muriel would offer to let them stay on with her, he'd warrant. Neither her son nor her daughter lived nearby, and, although she'd lick a blacksmith's anvil before admitting it, she was lonely. "And you can bet your brass buttons the rumor mills will churn furiously if we wed so hastily when I've only been back in England a week."

The tattlemongers would have a glorious time of it

in any event.

"He's right, Giles. You can take to your bed while we wait, and I'm sure, as my future husband, Bradford wouldn't deny you the best possible medical care." Philomena flashed Bradford a fleeting glance, a challenge in the angle of her head. Probably sparking in her eyes, too. "Why, you might make a full recovery. Three weeks isn't so very long."

By far the oddest proposal and acceptance he'd ever heard of. Perhaps she hoped to buy time with the delay. For what? Another suitor? Pomfrett to change his mind? His health to improve?

Time to get to know her future husband, dolt?

"Three weeks ... *is* too long." A violent bout of coughing seized Pomfrett. One hand covering his mouth, he fumbled about in his coat pocket, his shoulders shaking.

Philomena passed him her handkerchief, her face as pale as the lace-edged cloth. "Here. Use mine."

A few moments passed before he stopped hacking and pulled the kerchief from his mouth. He quickly crumpled the strip into a wad, but not before Bradford saw the scarlet splotches. Her attention remained fixed on her brother's hand holding the telltale stained handkerchief.

She'd seen the blotches too.

The anguished, pleading gaze she turned on Bradford tore his heart from his chest. "Can you ... I know you wanted to wait, but would you please consider seeing the Archbishop tomorrow about the license? To at least have it on hand?"

"I—"

Two half-foxed young bucks stumbled into the enclosure.

"Say, wot's this? A lovers' tryst?" A stout fellow with a neck so short his chins appeared to rest upon his thick shoulders snickered and elbowed his cohort. Tilting his head, he took a lengthy swallow from his flask. An equally long belch followed, sending him into another fit of chortling. He clomped forward, flask extended toward his friend. "Care for a nip?"

"No, and don't be daft, Henderson. That's Pomfrett and his sister." The fop's gaze scraped Philomena head to toe before narrowing to slits upon spying Bradford. The drunken coxcomb slid her a sly smile. "Or perhaps, something *is* afoot."

Bradford straightened, forcing the cull to crane his neck to meet his eyes.

"Nothing of the sort. The Pomfretts and I are old friends, and I am the most fortunate of men that Miss Pomfrett has just agreed to become my viscountess, honoring a promise made many years ago."

"You don't say?" The portly chap slapped the other on the back. "I won that bet, Underhill. Told you she had her sights set higher than a fourth son, I did. And you said no one of upper worth would have her. Calls for a celebration, it does."

Philomena bristled and impaled Underhill with her narrowed eyes.

Maggot.

Bradford itched to plant the boor a facer. He wasn't fit to wipe her slippers on.

Henderson quaffed another long swallow from his flask. The stench of strong spirits emanated from him, and Bradford's nostrils twitched. Seems the bosky chap had been celebrating a great deal this evening.

Underhill scowled at his chum before striking a superior pose and elevating his nose. "Rather poor form, encouraging a gentleman's attentions when you're already promised to another, Miss Pomfrett. I admit to being quite put upon. The *ton* doesn't tolerate such fast and fickle behavior."

Bradford clenched his fists. Only uneasiness about Philomena's reaction kept him from bloodying Underhill's nose.

"The only thing fast and fickle in this arbor is you, Mr. Underhill. You flit from silly girl to silly girl quicker than a bee after nectar, always with the intent of relieving her of her dowry and virginity, and not necessarily in that order. I am not such an empty-headed ninnyhammer and never once encouraged your attentions." Philomena stood and gave the fop a frosty stare, clutching her fan as if she'd like to give him a good poke.

The Philomena of old would have.

Another chilly breeze blew past, sending the greenery to quivering, and she hugged herself, shivering. Though mild for a May evening, the temperature

had dipped in the last half hour, a not-so-subtle reminder that spring hadn't yet lost winter's sting.

"If you were already spoken for, why did your
brother go about practically begging men to take you
off his hands?" Underhill's reedy voice exploded into
the stunned silence.

"That's outside of enough, you lying, ill-begotten
swine." Giles lurched to his feet, his sister immediately
scooting to his side and restraining him. "Apologize to
my sister—"

Damn it to hell.

Seizing Underhill's lapels, Bradford jerked him off
the ground. He gave a sharp shake, satisfaction
thrumming through him. Underhill provided just the
outlet he needed for his pent-up emotions. "You will
apologize to the future Viscountess Kingsley and her
brother, and then take your sorry arse and leave. Is that
understood?"

Bullies like Underhill seldom stood up to bolder
men.

Underhill gulped audibly, his toady eyes bulging.
His mouth worked, but no lucid sound emerged for a

few seconds. At last, he managed a strangled, "Yes. Quite. My lord."

"Viscountess Kingsley? Thought I heard my cousin tittering something about a Viscountess Kingsley. Cannot 'member what, 'xactly." Henderson scratched his chins and squinted at Bradford. "Victoria does prattle on 'bout the queerest things. Spent a quarter of an hour discussin' various shades of yellow embroidery thread last time I saw the gel. She had seventeen. I try m' best to ignore her."

Babbling must be a family trait.

Bradford lowered Underhill until his feet settled on the pavers. Keeping one hand firmly round his arm, Bradford propelled the bufflehead toward Philomena and Giles, each looking ready to topple head over bum.

"Please accept my deepest, most earnest apology, Miss Pomfrett, Pomfrett." Underhill's grudging mutter, steeped in insincerity, clearly conveyed the opposite.

Not bloody good enough. Not by half. Bradford jerked Underhill's upper arm. "And?"

Underhill's brows crashed together in an irate glower. "I was completely out of order and unaccountably rude."

"And?" Bradford intended to wring every drop of remorse from the cur for insulting Philomena.

Underhill shot Bradford a venom-laced glare. "I humbly beg your forgiveness."

"And?"

As he swung to face Bradford, Underhill's face contorted into a snarl. "What the bloody hell else am I supposed to say?"

Bradford chuckled, quite enjoying taking this uppity cawker down a peg.

"That you're a foul-mouthed, thoughtless chucklehead who's undeserving of a woman as magnificent as Miss Pomfrett, and that she even deigns to be in the same room with a twiddlepoop such as you is an honor beyond measure."

"Chucklehead. Twiddlepoop." Henderson released a girlish giggle, his flask at the ready once more. He hiccupped. "'Pon my rep, tha'ssh funny."

"Stubble it, Henderson." Huffing his displeasure, Underhill wheeled round to face Philomena again. "I'm a thoughtless—"

"Giles?" Philomena's husky voice rose in alarm. "Bradford!"

Bradford lunged too late.

Pomfrett hit the ground with a portentous thud.

5

Fate proved most fickle, bestowing a welcome blessing after extracting an excruciating toll. Philomena could find no other explanation for her and Giles staying in the Duchess of Daventry's luxurious home while he battled for his life.

The duchess's wholly unexpected generosity and kindness knew no bounds. Immediately upon spying Bradford carrying Giles's limp form into Wimpleton's manor, she'd sailed to the entrance, called for her coach, and insisted Giles be transported to her much closer house rather than the humble—more aptly, tumbledown—cottage Philomena and Giles rented on London's outskirts. The colorful dame had also sent for her personal physician and insisted on paying Doctor

Singleton's fee as well.

"You're my guests, Miss Pomfrett. I won't hear another word about paying Singleton. That crusty, old barnacle ought to tend your brother for free considering how frequently I've needed his services of late." She'd winked, a mischievous youthful glint in her eyes, despite the wrinkles etching her once handsome face. "Aging is not for the faint of heart."

"I'm sure that is true," Philomena murmured politely, uncertain what else to say.

"Besides, I quite anticipate seeing my nephew at sixes and sevens with you underfoot. That cocksure boy could do with a good rattling. I remember how eagerly he anticipated visits to Bromhamshire, my dear, and I know it wasn't anticipation of seeing his cantankerous uncle or wastrel cousins at Bromham Hall that had him gallivanting to the country at every opportunity."

With a painful pang to the region near her heart, Philomena remembered too. Blinking back tears, she forced her lips to turn up. She couldn't retrace her steps and relive the past few years. Her only choice was to move forward, wherever that obscure path might lead her. "I'm not positive his lordship's affections are what they once were, Your Grace."

"Hmph. More fool he then." The duchess's expression grew solemn, though kindness brimmed in her eyes. "My dear, if things shouldn't work out between you and my nephew, I would be honored if you would consider becoming my companion. My son's wife prefers that I not visit often, and once Olivia marries ... well, this drafty old house gets lonely. And I dearly want to visit my daughter in Spain but have hesitated to take the journey by myself."

Glad tears blurred Philomena's eyes. An answer to one prayer. "Your offer is very generous, Your Grace, and one I gratefully accept."

"Excellent. You've made me very happy, though in truth, I hope that boy comes to his senses." After kissing Philomena's cheek, her grace had set off to the kitchen to ensure a hearty broth was prepared in the event Giles awoke.

Now, whether he lived or died, Philomena wasn't compelled to wed. Profoundly relieved, the closest thing to peace she'd experienced in long while engulfed her. She smoothed the rich satin counterpane across his chest again, then—holding her breath—tentatively rested her palm upon his gaunt chest. Yes, he still breathed, though shallow and weak, his lips blue tinged and his pallor as white as the sheets he lay upon.

Ten days he'd lain here, rarely rousing. Ten trying, yet wonderful, days as Giles struggled for his life, and she and Bradford became reacquainted. Fate's capriciousness again, bringing Philomena's only love back into her life just as she faced losing her brother.

She'd fallen in love with Bradford all over again. More accurately, she'd never stopped loving him, but in recent days, she had dared to allow the emotion she'd deliberately buried so long ago, to reemerge—perhaps foolishly, and she would regret her lapse later. Her love had grown and bloomed into something wondrous and magical, way beyond a young girl's adoration into the permanent binding of her soul to his.

How could it not? Loving him came as easily as the sun rising or rain falling.

There would be no other man for her. Ever.

He, on the other hand, had given no indication, not the merest hint, whether he returned her affection, and the uncertainty kept her lips sealed. Especially, since there'd been no further mention of them wedding either—not that she'd hold him to the absurd bargain Giles had negotiated, rather demanded, in the bower.

Nonetheless, that knowledge, added to her despair about Giles, had become an almost unbearable ache. She was at once, her happiest and gloomiest, a jumble of conflicting emotions.

Giles stirred, mumbling something incoherent before stilling once more. Only a trace remained of the purplish, egg-sized bump on his forehead and the ugly scrape along his left cheek from his tumble. With each new dawn, she praised God that he still lived.

A regretful half-smile tipped her mouth as she examined the chamber.

He'd never slept in finer bedding, yet he couldn't appreciate the quality of the luxurious ivory and gold coverlet or the opulent room. That couldn't be said of the Kingsleys' rotund, orange-striped tabby. Socrates, his nose tucked beneath a white-tipped paw, lay curled against Giles's legs, snoozing contentedly.

Sitting beside Giles, she lifted his limp hand and closed her eyes in silent prayer. *Please God.* She pressed the back to her cheek then kissed the cool flesh.

"You must get better, Giles. You're all I have. I know it's selfish of me, and would extend your suffering, but I cannot bear losing you. I'm not ready to be alone yet. It's too soon."

I shall never be ready. How can I let him go?

A tender touch to her shoulder made her eyelids fly open.

"You have me, Philomena."

Bradford had slipped into the chamber, leaving the door ajar. His taut-fitting emerald jacket emphasized the breadth of his wide shoulders, and his ivory pantaloons accentuated his ridiculously long, muscular legs. An emerald stickpin winked from the folds of his cravat, and sooty stubble shadowed his strong jaw. Was he one of those men who needed to shave twice daily? She longed to rub her cheek against the roughness and inhale his unique, manly scent.

Her heart turned over, or perhaps the peculiar fluttering centered in her stomach—so difficult to tell which, when her breath snagged and her pulse stumbled momentarily.

He'd never looked more striking, and a flash of awareness dampened her palms.

The youthful Bradford had been such a charming scamp. The mature man, a dangerously rakish rogue. Both had captivated her heart, although the latter proved the more formidable.

He'd always been deft of foot and used to creep into the vicarage's gardens too. He relished surprising her with a new ribbon, a handful of posies, a book, or even on occasion, *La Bell Assembleé* or *Ackermann's Repository* he'd filched from his mother.

How Philomena had delighted in perusing Ackermann's fashion plates and reading the latest *on dit*. And gleaning every useful morsel that might help her be a wife worthy of him when the day finally came. Moisture pooled in her eyes as much for the loss of their innocent, uncomplicated love as for her brother.

"Do I have you, even though Giles meant to co-erce you into wedding me?" She searched Bradford's face. How she adored him.

Compassion deepened his eyes to midnight blue. His handsome mouth tilted sympathetically, and he squeezed her shoulder, leaving his sturdy hand there, the possessive gesture infusing her with his strength. "You always have and always shall."

Unbidden warmth welled in her chest, spiraling outward, the heat spreading into her veins, giving her hope. Did he mean it? Could he truly care for her still?

Had time diminished her feelings for him?

No, but unlike a besotted schoolgirl blinded by giddiness, a woman clearly recognized love's poignan-cy and fallibility, and the risk it took to surrender one-self to the emotion. To love with abandon meant relin-quishing part of your soul to another, trusting unre-servedly. The pain she'd endured when she thought Bradford had betrayed her had been a thousand times worse than her burn-ravaged flesh, and she never wanted to endure that agony again.

She wouldn't survive.

To hide the maelstrom of regret assailing her, Philomena busied herself tucking Giles's hand under the bedding, atop his chest. After smoothing the covers once more, she plucked the faded gingham skirt of the well-worn dress Bradford had retrieved from her cottage this morning.

"Thank you for this. I'm rather self-conscious about others seeing my scars, else I would have gratefully accepted Olivia's sweet offer to borrow a gown."

Which would have been several inches too long, and probably too snug around as well. Olivia sported a tall, lithesome figure, whereas Philomena was of average height and much rounder curves shaped her form.

"Understandable." His attention dipped to her chest for a fraction, no doubt curious what, precisely, the gown hid. Except the appreciative gleam in his eyes gave her pause. Mayhap he speculated about something other than the scars, and for the first time since the flames had ravaged her flesh, womanly awareness puckered her breasts.

His penetrating gaze again swooped downward again. Could he see the pebble-hard tips? "Do they bother you?"

My nipples?

"Do they hurt?"

Not hurt exactly, more of an ache.

Jaw slack, and in an unaccustomed dither, Philomena struggled for an appropriate answer. How did one respond to a gentleman discussing your bosoms?

A set down and a sharp slap, that's how. She couldn't muster the vexation for either, or more on point, didn't want to. His impertinence should outrage her, and that it didn't revealed just how deeply, and absolutely he'd captured her. Again.

"I beg your pardon." His gaze snared hers before he rolled his head, his sheepish expression that of a rascally child who knew he'd overstepped the bounds. "That was much too forward. I but worried the scars yet caused you discomfort."

"Oh."

See, nincompoop. He wasn't talking about your breasts at all.

Thank goodness she hadn't scolded him. His intent had been solicitousness. Then why did she feel mildly disappointed he hadn't been ogling her? She raised a shoulder and fingered a loose thread at her wrist. "They itch at times, and I dislike how they feel when I touch them. I don't think I shall ever become accustomed."

She wouldn't. Would he or any other man? How could she expect them to?

That was one reason she'd been reluctant to encourage her undesirable suitors, despite her promise to Giles. Nevertheless, she retained the smallest iota of hope that a man would yearn to wed her and not be disgusted by her scars. If only that man could be Bradford.

"I imagine it would take time." No hint of distaste registered on his face or in his deep voice, only sympathy. "Are there many?"

"Several. You do know the viscount started the fire?" Focusing on a Blue John vase atop the fireplace mantel beyond his shoulder, she relived the horror. The scorching heat and acrid smoke. The agony and the terror. She veered Bradford a sideways glance. "Giles told me he confronted him. Your uncle claimed he accidentally dropped a candle near the altar when he kneeled to pray."

"That damn—" Nostrils flaring and jaw taut, Bradford smothered the vulgar curse.

He needn't on her behalf, for she had condemned Herbert Kingsley to every kind of hell imaginable, particularly in those first horrendous weeks. She hadn't forgiven him entirely either, perhaps never would be able to. Every glimpse of herself unclothed in a mirror reminded her of her parents' needless deaths, Giles's suffering, and the loss of Bradford's love. She rolled a shoulder in an attempt at graciousness. "Perhaps he truly had sought God's guidance."

"What utter rot." Bradford took a deep breath. "Forgive me, but my uncle hadn't set foot in a church for decades, and if that spawn of Satan prayed, it wasn't to God Almighty, I assure you."

"I supposed as much." Nodding, she blinked drowsily.

Sleep had eluded her these past weeks. Anxiety for Giles, apprehension about their finances, and dread of an inevitable marriage robbed her of slumber nightly.

Though she needn't worry about the latter two any-more, Giles's condition still kept her tossing and turn-ing. She yawned behind her hand, weary to her bones' marrow. "I've always wondered why he hated us so."

"That we'll never know." Bradford cupped her nape and rubbed her knotted neck muscles, the long strokes and gentle kneading bringing much-needed re-lief. "How does Giles fare? Any improvement?"

"No." She shook her head. "Though, he's no worse either."

Bradford made a short sound in the back of his throat. "I had hoped for better news, for your sake."

For the life of her, she couldn't form a single pro-test at his impudence, or the impropriety of his caress-es, but instead, closed her eyes and bowed her neck, breathing out a silent sigh. She'd missed his touch, and like a long-parched plant, soaked the sensation into every arid pore.

"That's it. Relax. You deserve a modicum of res-pite. You're half asleep on your feet." He brushed her hair aside—tied back with a ribbon rather than knotted properly atop her head—

before setting both hands to massaging her neck and shoulders.

Could he feel the few irregular, hardened ridges through her dress's thin fabric? The worst scars, the ribbons of unsightly, rigid flesh, marred her front and her upper arms. She sighed as errant flickers pulsed in places she had no business noticing with her dying brother lying beside her, and she shifted, edging away from Bradford.

Socrates raised his head and, citrine orbs barely open, eyed her disdainfully for disturbing his nap before yawning and resuming his slumber.

"When was Doctor Singleton last here?" Bradford's voice, velvety and warm, hinted that touching her had affected him too.

Examining the bedside clock, she frowned.

Three o'clock already? Where had the day gone?

Her stomach rumbled and contracted. She'd forgotten to eat from the tray a servant had brought up hours ago. "He was here just after twelve, and said he would return this evening with different medication."

Bradford pulled an armchair up beside the bed

and, after flipping his tails out of the way, took a seat. He rummaged in his pocket, and his mouth edged upward as he removed a velvet case.

When she didn't reach for it, he set the box on her thigh. "Here."

"What is it?" A jolt of awareness spiraled outward. Philomena eyed the maroon square guardedly.

"A betrothal ring. It belonged to my grandmother, and Aunt Muriel was adamant you should have it." He gave her another lopsided grin and arched a raven brow. "One does not tell the duchess no."

Definitely not. Philomena's mouth twitched into a nascent smile. "Yes, I gathered that, but she is a dear, if somewhat formidable."

"If you don't like the style, we can purchase another." He patted his coat, his signet ring flashing in the candlelight. "I have the special license, too, and I have arranged for a cleric to perform the ceremony." A grin lit his eyes, the same deep azure of the horizon at sunset. "I even found a suitable house to rent until we can find something permanent to purchase. It's small but will suffice for now."

He had a license as well? Her heart somersaulted. And found a place for them to live? Happiness embraced her. He meant to honor what he said in the arbor? Giddiness capered atop her ribs. She couldn't have known. He hadn't spoken of it.

He hadn't mentioned love either.

Doubt poked its beastly head up, quashing her internal celebration.

Did Bradford want to marry her, or did guilt and obligation compel him?

Her joy plunged to her scuffed half-boots, and lay there wallowing pathetically. He mustn't marry her out of duty or a misplaced sense of honor and forgo his chance at love. She must tell him, make him understand that it was all right if he didn't wed her. She would be fine.

Turning, she faced him square on.

"Bradford, you don't have to marry me. I know I'm not your first choice, and now that Giles is ..." She blinked away the fresh sting of tears and swallowed past the lump clogging her throat. "Well, not meeting anyone on the field of honor anytime soon, there's really no need to bother to see this through to the end. I do thank you for the noble gesture, nonetheless."

Though curiosity screeched in umbrage at being denied a glimpse of the ring, she placed the unopened jewelry box in his palm. Better not to know, for all that stood between her disintegrating into a weeping ninny was an eyelash's width of pride.

Bradford stared at the case for a long moment before lifting his thick-lashed eyes to hers, and her heart gave a painful flip. Love shouldn't be simultaneously agonizing and glorious.

Unblinking, he looked at her.

She could get lost in those beautiful pools. He'd always had the most vivid eyes, and his lashes caused many a lady to jealously gnash her teeth.

"Philomena, I know we haven't seen each other in almost seven years, and much has happened in our lives to change us. But, these last days, I thought ... had begun to believe ..." He pointed his attention ceilingward and puffed out a short breath. "Isn't there even a spark of what we once had?"

"I ... I don't know. Yes. Maybe. Probably."

Liar. You know blasted well there is.

Pressing her fingertips to her temples, she strove to order her scattered thoughts. "It's more complicated than that. I'm not sure we can simply resume where we left off."

She could, but could he?

Did he love her?

"I truly did not know you lived." He took her hand and entwined their fingers like he used to. So natural and comfortable. "I was almost grateful Father decided to drag us off to the Caribbean, because it meant escaping England and the memories of you. They haunted me, tortured me, nearly driving me mad."

"You truly grieved for me?" Searching his striking face, the planes harsh with remembered sorrow, her resolve slipped.

Shutting his eyes, he compressed his lips and gave a terse nod. "For months. Years." His deep voice rumbled, and he opened his eyes, a glint of moisture confirming his words. Pressing her hand to his firm lips, he murmured against her palm, "I wanted to die."

Needing to comfort him, Philomena brushed a

lone droplet from the corner of his eye and offered a tremulous smile as she caressed his cheek. "Hurts bloody awful, doesn't it?"

"Most excruciating thing I've ever endured." Bradford bent nearer, until inches separated their mouths, the smoldering smile on his lips only slightly less heated than the scorching luster in his eye.

Sliding her hand to the back of his head, Philomena smiled. She spread her fingers in his silky hair and pulled him closer. "Me too."

His lips settled on hers, and she wrapped her arms around his neck, clinging to him. This kiss, each nibble and touch of their tongues, spoke of sorrow and forgiveness and pledged healing and hope. Their mouths meshed, she scooted onto his firm lap and gave herself over to the experience, reveling in the momentary joy.

A pillow softly smacked her.

6

After wresting her mouth from Bradford's, Philomena leapt to her feet. "Giles, you're awake!"

"A man cannot even die in peace. He must rouse to defend his sister's honor."

Heat swept up the angles of her cheeks at being caught kissing Bradford again, but she returned Giles's feeble grin.

"How long have I been out?"

Philomena grasped his hand, her mouth quivering. "Ten days. I feared you'd never waken."

Giles's turbid gaze locked on Bradford. His focus sank lower, to the jewelry box still clasped in Bradford's hand. "You said you had retained a cleric?"

Hands on her hips and lips pursed, Philomena angled her head. "Just how much of our conversation did you eavesdrop on? And why didn't you tell me ... us," she spared Bradford a swift glance, "you were awake?"

"One cannot eavesdrop on a conversation taking place over one's deathbed." Giles's lips bent into a tired smile. "As for not telling you I'd awoken, I found the conversation most fascinating, and truthfully, it took too much effort to open my eyes or speak."

"I do hope you don't intend to call me out again." Bradford winked and patted Giles's shoulder.

"If I weren't so relieved, Giles Joseph Pomfrett, I would ring you a peal, you sneak." Philomena smiled through her tears and kissed his cheek. She'd never thought to hear his voice or see the playful gleam in his eye again.

Dark circles ringing his bleary eyes, he struggled into a sitting position, his gaze wavering between her and Bradford. "You still love each other?"

"I ..." She sent Bradford a helpless glance. Why must that be one of the first things Giles asked upon waking?

"I love her. I always have." Bradford's voice entwined around her heart. "Even more so these past few days as we've become reacquainted—not that we needed to. We resumed right where we left off, didn't we, Phil?"

She took the hand he extended, the answering warmth in his eyes turning her knees to custard. "Yes, and I do love him. But I think you suspected that, brother dearest."

The tiniest twinkle glinted in Giles's eyes. "I but hoped and played the hand as if you did. I nearly danced a jig when I came upon Kingsley kissing you in the arbor. Quite opportune, I must say."

"That was well done of you, Giles." Bradford brushed a tendril from Philomena's cheek that had escaped her ribbon when they kissed. "And that's why I asked Reverend Archer to pay a call at four o'clock to discuss the ceremony. Quite by chance, I met the man of God at a dinner party when I first returned to London, and when I came upon him today after obtaining the marriage license, I asked him to officiate."

"Yes, that was fortuitous." Moments ago, she'd been moping about because there'd been no mention of marriage, and now she was aflutter at the suddenness of Bradford's arrangements.

He gave Philomena an apologetic smile. "Forgive

me for not discussing this with you, but the Archbishop just returned to London last evening, and I honestly didn't expect to encounter Reverend Archer today. Things just fell into place, and I snatched the opportunity while it was available."

"Phil, Kingsley has the license, and you love each other. Why not simply marry when the rector arrives?" Giles's question sent her pulse stampeding uncomfortably.

Four o'clock today?

She would have preferred a bit more notice to prepare.

"I cannot be married in this old rag. I must change, and arrange my hair." Glancing downward, Philomena grasped her dress and grimaced. Chagrined, she darted Bradford a hesitant glance and sighed. "You must think me vain and silly."

He cupped her chin. "What's wrong with wanting our wedding to be as special as we can make it?"

"I cannot suitably express my gratitude or what a balm to my soul it is to know Philomena is provided for after I'm gone." Giles extended a trembling hand, which Bradford promptly clasped. "I can rest peacefully now."

Philomena's heart gave a queer leap. His words rang with a resignation and finality she'd not heard before. "Giles, don't talk like that. You may still grow stronger."

"Bradford." A scratching at the door preceded the Duchess of Daventry sailing into the room, followed by Olivia and a twitchy little man of the cloth. "Reverend Archer requests a word with you."

"You're early, Reverend." Bradford beamed, nonetheless.

"Yes, your lordship, if you please." The reverend ducked his head and wrung his hands, moisture edging his upper lip. "Perhaps we could step into the corridor?"

Olivia sped to Philomena's side and, after embracing her, hugged Bradford. "I'm so happy for you both. Brady has often teased me about my doldrums over Allen, but do believe me when I tell you, Philomena, he was much changed after the fire." Bestowing a bright smile on Giles, Olivia touched his shoulder. "And I'm so grateful you've roused, Mr. Pomfrett. I will pray for your continued recovery."

The strain of so many gathered in Giles's sick room concerned Philomena. She would wait until the doctor examined him before she allowed the dash of hope that had taken root to grow and bloom. Too soon for celebrating, just yet. Nonetheless, his awakening in time for the ceremony was a profound blessing.

Her grace regarded the cleric with thinly disguised curiosity but turned her attention to Giles. "I'm so pleased to see you awake, Mr. Pomfrett. You shall have the pleasure of witnessing your sister's nuptials, though I do believe we should make the ceremony as short as possible so as to not exhaust you."

"Er, well, Your Grace, there is a small matter I need to discuss with his lordship first." The cleric's nervous gaze darted here and there, and perspiration ran in thick rivets down his beet-red face. As quickly as he sopped the moisture with his soggy kerchief, more appeared.

Goodness, he appeared unwell or on the brink of apoplexy.

"Have your say, good sir, so that we might be about marrying." Bradford encircled Philomena's waist with one arm. "I've waited nearly seven years to marry this minx, and don't want to wait another day."

"You are going to have to wait, my lord." Reverend Archer clasped his hands, his head bobbing like a pigeon.

Bradford stiffened and leveled him an acerbic stare. "And why is that?"

Every eye in the room fixed on the clergyman.

He licked his lips and tugged on his ear. "Someone has come forth with an objection to the marriage."

Her ocean-blue eyes rounded, Olivia grasped Philomena's hand. "I am so sorry, Philomena."

Henderson and Underhill had wasted no time in spreading the news of Bradford's betrothal claim, it seemed. And someone, though God only knew who, didn't want Bradford and her to wed. Well, actually, she could think of several hungry-eyed women who wouldn't be pleased, but none had legal reason to protest the joining.

She pressed two fingers between her eyebrows where a steady cadence thrummed.

"Who dares?" Her grace narrowed her eyes to incensed slits and shook her finger in the reverend's face, causing the man to blanch and stumble backward. "I'll see they are banned from every respectable assembly. They won't be able to nibble Sally Lunn's cake with anyone of refinement by the time I'm finished. They'll be buying their vegetables from the slop yard."

Bradford maintained a visage of calm, though anger tempered his speech. "What's this about? Unless they are here to state their objection during the ceremony, they can caterwaul and complain from the rooftops and it will do no good."

"Your uncle entered into a contract with Lord Southwark, agreeing his daughter would be the next Viscountess Kingsley." After taking a deep breath, the cleric hurried on, running his words together. "The-late-viscount-accepted-the marriage-settlement-and-the–terms-stipulated-the joining-occur-before-Parliament's-dissolution."

Her grace released a snort worthy of an incensed bull. "Figures. Raynott Southwark's a covetous, ambitious fribble. And that bland-eyed daughter of his has more hair than wit." The duchess made a circular gesture near her temple. "She's not all there in the attic. Simple-minded, the unfortunate dear."

The poor girl was a slow top, but this had nothing to do with Bradford and Philomena's wedding.

"Easily remedied." Bradford flashed a reassuring smile, completely unaffected by the reverend's announcement. "I shall return the settlement since my cousins are deceased. However, as my future brother-in-law's health is extremely delicate, we'll proceed with the nuptials as planned."

Philomena released her pent-up breath. A simple misunderstanding brought about by the prior viscount's untimely death. In truth, she wouldn't object to a short courting period, a few weeks delay to further reacquaint herself with the man she had pledged to marry, but Giles's health made that impossible.

"Yes, it is my brother's express wish that Bradford and I marry as quickly as possible." She couldn't bring herself to say because Giles might not live to see the deed done if they delayed.

"I'm dying, Reverend, and would see my sister wed before I leave this world." Giles wearily shut his eyes, and poignant silence reigned for a long moment.

"I understand, and you have my utmost sympathy, but the matter isn't so easily rectified." The reverend fussed with his collar, his face glowing. How was it possible for a human to turn the same hue as a parrot's plumage? "The contract doesn't specify or identify *which* viscount Lady Victoria is to marry."

Philomena exchanged a baffled glance with Olivia. Why did the man persist? He obviously knew Bradford wasn't party to any of these legalities, and what difference did it make whether the agreement identified the viscount? Everyone knew it couldn't be Bradford. He'd been out of the country until just over a fortnight ago and was last in line to inherit, to boot.

"Speak clearly, man. What are you saying, exactly?" Bradford's countenance settled into sharply hewn angles. Though not easily riled, his patience appeared at an end.

The cleric gulped and sucked in a large breath. "Simply put, the contract states that Viscount Kingsley will join with the Lady Victoria Southwark within one week of Parliament's recessing."

"**P**reposterous and unenforceable."

Bradford shook his head and flipped open the jewelry box. He removed the garnet circled in seed pearls and held it up. The crimson jewel glittered in the candlelight, a vivid flash of hope amongst darkness and despair. "I mean to marry Philomena."

"But, my lord—"

"Nothing this side of the Good Lord descending from heaven and trussing me like a turkey will stop me." Undeterred, he slid the ring onto her slender finger. "And even then, He and I would have a fierce go round."

"Blasphemous." Reverend Archer sputtered, shaking his finger at Bradford. "You should do penance for such profane irreverence."

"Nonsense. I have no intention of martyring myself by marrying a chit I've never met to preserve family honor I didn't taint."

Uncle Herbert could bugger on in his grave, and Southwark could work his wiles somewhere else. No erroneous sense of duty compelled Bradford to toddle down the aisle with an insipid stranger. Not now that his beloved Phil had been returned to him.

"It's quite exquisite." Philomena fingered the slightly loose ring, wonder and disbelief, wreathing her face.

He'd been drowning in similar sentiment since discovering she lived and wasn't about to let her escape him this time.

Another emotion lingered on her features as well. He looked closely. Yes, there about her eyes. Discomfit? Uncertainty? About what?

Women of Philomena's ilk were rare and irreplaceable, and she was so entangled in his being that, for the first time in a great while, he felt whole once more. Marry her first, then worry how they'd get on, for if he lost her again, he'd become a shell of a man with nothing to live for.

Besides, they loved each other, and this past week and a half had been the happiest he'd experienced in the past seven years. Everything about her fascinated and enthralled him, and he held no doubts that his love for her would only grow.

"It belonged to my mother, Bradford and Olivia's grandmother. She was a Prussian princess, you know." A faraway look entered Aunt Muriel's eyes. "Now that's a lovely story. Father rode his stallion right into church, swept her onto the saddle, and kissing her passionately, galloped away. The gossip was deliciously scandalous."

"I'd like to know how Grandpapa managed the kiss, the horse's reins, and the pews all at once. Some feat, that. Were his eyes closed? I always kiss with my eyes closed." Bradford's quip earned him a dark look.

"Do shut-up, Bradford." Aunt Muriel motioned toward the ring, the tiniest hint of censure pulling her mouth downward. "Daventry's bride wanted something more modern—to the tune of five hundred pounds more—my Isobel was gifted a familial ring from her husband, and Olivia has her mother's ring, one similar to the garnet." Vulnerability bathed her expression for an instant. "I understand if you prefer your own, but I thought for today's ceremony ..."

Now cancelled for lack of a clergyman.

Caressing the ring, Philomena shook her head. "Your Grace ..."

"Pooh, none of that nonsense." Aunt Muriel flapped her hand as if trying to swat a pigeon-sized fly. "We're to be family. Aunt Muriel, please."

"Aunt Muriel." Philomena's pretty mouth bent upward. "I am honored beyond measure you would gift me with something so precious."

Aunt Muriel beamed and tutted a bit, before surreptitiously patting the corner of her eye.

Philomena's compassionate gaze met Bradford's.

No, by God, nothing and no one had better attempt to keep him from taking this thoughtful, enchanting woman to wife.

"Sir, perhaps you should view the agreement?" Archer shifted from foot to foot, not quite daring to meet his eyes.

Hand on his hips, Bradford curled his lips contemptuously. "My uncle may have thought himself clever, but that contract is worthless and will not stand legal examination. No one with a modicum of common sense would expect me to honor it."

"Hence why that lackwit, Southwark, thinks you will." Aunt Muriel ran ringed fingers over the drowsy cat, now sprawled on his back, purring. "The man's not given to common sense."

"That may be, sir, but I cannot, in good conscience, perform the ceremony." The cleric half-turned to the door, reminding Bradford of a cockroach scuttling back to its hidey-hole. "You may encounter difficulty in finding someone to marry you until you clarify you are not already betrothed, my lord."

"Humph, sounds suspiciously like a threat to me, you little weasel. Southwark probably greased a scoundrel's fist to spy on my nephew and follow him around with orders to report back when Bradford saw the archbishop." Aunt Muriel stomped to the cowering parson, giving him a crushing glare.

"Is that why I just happened to run into you, Reverend?" Bradford stepped forward a pair of paces, threateningly. Would he burn in hell for shaking a man of God until his teeth clacked?

"Isn't Southwark part of your congregation? Which did he do?" Aunt Muriel prodded the man of God's chest none-too-gently. "Bribe you to not perform the ceremony, or threatened to take his patronage elsewhere, you grasping little toad-eater?"

Archer, quailing under her scowl, recoiled as if shot and bumped into the bed.

Lord, but Bradford admired his spirited aunt.

Socrates flopped onto his stomach and, letting loose a reproachful yowl, swatted the reverend's back end. Archer howled and jumped, grabbing his injured buttock.

Bradford chuckled.

Liked his sister's damn cat, too.

"Undoubtedly he did both, the wretch. Probably hovered about like a bat waiting for Bradford to approach his eminence." Philomena regarded the cleric with the same favor she would a piece of moldy fruit.

"Despicable behavior from a man of the cloth."

"How do you live with yourself? As a representative of God's house, you should be above such unscrupulousness." Reprove curled Olivia's mouth and narrowed her gaze.

The color drained from Reverend Archer's face, and he swiped a hand across his beaded brow. With a show of bravado, he thrust his scrawny chest out and lifted his nose. "I am a servant of God, and I resent your scurrilous accusations."

"Scurrilous? Surprised he even knows the word," Giles mumbled, cracking his eyelids open for an instant. "How about charlatan and fraud? Pharisee?"

Archer pursed his thin lips, giving Giles a haughty look. "Have a care, sir. You should be asking for absolution, not tossing names at God's appointed servant." He turned his disapproving, bug-eyed scrutiny on Philomena. "The Church takes a dim view of hasty marriages. Perhaps, if you spent more time on your knees in prayer rather than aspiring to a station above you and making plans to gallivant off on a honeymoon when your brother lies dying—"

"Rubbish and rot!" Aunt Muriel claimed the cleric's elbow and hauled him to the door. With a less then gentle shove, she thrust him over the threshold.

Damn good thing she'd reached Archer before Bradford did. He itched to break the cleric's bulbous nose or ring his skinny neck.

Philomena canted her head, her gaze shooting green daggers. "And what is the Church's view on corrupt, immoral clerics?"

"Mayfield." Aunt Muriel bellowed for the butler. "I'm clearing the premises of vermin. Show Reverend Archer the door." Before the majordomo arrived, she slammed the door in Archer's flabbergasted face then swung round to face the others. "I know a rat when I smell one."

"What now?" Philomena folded her arms and thrummed the fingertips of one hand on her arm. Not precisely fretful, but not unaffected either. Truthfully, she appeared quite agitated.

Aunt Muriel waggled her eyebrows and rubbed her hands together gleefully. "It's very simple. Bradford cries off."

"I do?" Understanding dawned. "Indeed. I do!"

His long gait carried him across the room to his grinning aunt. Giving her an exuberant hug, he laughed in delight. "Oh, the scandal! The cut directs. The *on dit*. Marvelous. We'll be ostracized. I can retire to the country and retain someone respectable to sit in my place in Parliament. What a fortuitous development."

"Bradford's not overly found of the *beau monde* set." Aunt Muriel's droll observation earned her another embrace.

"He rather likes to stir the waters, if you take my meaning." Olivia's eyes danced with amusement. "At times, it proves most offputting, and I wonder that I call him brother at all."

"Don't try to frighten my bride away with your flimflam." Striding to Philomena, he extended his hands. "I've never hidden my disdain for those affecting superior airs."

"I remember." At once, she gracefully rose and grasped his fingers.

Nevertheless, he detected the merest hint of reticence amid the eyes gazing so trustingly back at him.

What went on in her head? She had always been one to speak her mind before. But then, she'd suffered greatly, still did for her brother, and misery altered a person. He knew that full well. "Tell me, darling, would you be terribly put out with me if we didn't remain in London?"

A beatific smile swept her features, her nose crinkling adorably in more enthusiasm than he'd seen since their reunion. "Not at all. I'm more suited to country life, in truth. I've seen as many fops, dandies, coxcombs, and supposed ladies acting the part of light skirts than I care to in a lifetime."

"There is still the matter of marriage. If the reverend spoke true, and I believe he did, Southwark has likely made the rounds and intimidated all the clerics who are malleable." Giles tiredly rubbed his beard-stubbled jaw. "We are new to Town as well, and I haven't any idea whom to approach."

"You could elope to Scotland." Shrugging, Olivia gave a tight, apologetic smile. "If all else fails, that is."

"But that means leaving Giles." Philomena sank onto her brother's bed, and after giving him a falsely cheerful smile, clasped his hand. Her expression took on a stubborn set.

There's the old Philomena.

"I cannot go to Scotland, Bradford. I'm sorry."

"Of course we won't. It shall not come to that." Giving a sage nod, he drew his brows together in concentration and paced beside the bed, rubbing his chin. He swiveled in his aunt's direction. "Surely there is an honest cleric in all of London. If not, then a neighboring town."

"I have it." Aunt Muriel snapped her fingers, her expression exuberant. "I know a new vicar ... Alexander Hawksworth. He's the rector of a large parish outside London. Knew his father and mother. Much too handsome for a man of the cloth. His church pews don't stand empty on Sunday mornings, I can tell you. Though, how the man can preach over the tittering, whispering, and indelicate display of bosoms, I'll never know."

Philomena cast Giles a troubled look. His grayish skin and hollow cheeks bespoke a man not long for this world. She exchanged a pained glance with Bradford.

When her brother passed, she would grieve profoundly. They'd be making arrangements for a different type of service in the near future unless God intervened and performed a miracle. Why did this decent man have to suffer an early death while lickspittles like Underhill went about their merry, depraved lives?

Knowing someone you loved would soon die was excruciating. Bradford had gone through this very thing with Father, yet, at least his sire had lived a goodly number of years. If only Bradford could spare her this anguish.

"Do you think he would be willing to perform the ceremony, Your Grace?" Toying with the ends of her hair, Philomena hid a yawn behind her hand. The slight slump of her shoulders and faint bluish shadows beneath her eyes revealed her exhaustion, no doubt the result of sleepless nights.

"Indeed." Aunt Muriel delivered a shrewd smile and secured her fringed shawl more firmly. "He and my son were wont to get into all manner of mischief together at university. Hawksworth isn't cut from the typical cleric's cloth. When his Anglican priest uncle hied off to Gretna Green with a French nun, Hawksworth was expected to fill his uncle's shoes. He did so, rather reluctantly, I might add. I would wager my favorite Maid of Honor tarts, Hawksworth would jump at the chance."

Olivia made for the door. "Well then, Aunt, let's see about penning him a letter. He sounds like such a fascinating fellow. I want to ask Allen if Reverend Hawksworth might officiate at our wedding too."

"How soon can he come?" Giles's hoarse question immediately sobered the atmosphere. Socrates chose that moment to crawl onto his chest and gently bat Giles's face. "Seems even this portly feline worries for me."

Touching her chin, Aunt Muriel pondered for a moment. "If I send the letter with a trusted footman immediately, perhaps tomorrow afternoon? I'm sorry, Mr. Pomfrett, but I cannot be positive Hawksworth will be in residence or able to leave at once. I will make certain he's made aware of the urgency of the situation, however. I can also send word about Town that I seek him. He may be frequenting one of the gentlemen clubs, and I believe he's particularly fond of the theater."

"I'd be very grateful, Your Grace. I worry that I may experience another episode and fall insensate again." Giles turned his head in Philomena's direction. "Promise me, Phil, if I do, you will proceed with the marriage."

Shutting her eyes, Philomena nodded, but her lashes trembled against her cheeks. Poor darling. This ugliness had taken quite a toll on her. He couldn't help but think rushing into matrimony added more strain, even if they were in love.

"A moment, Aunt Muriel, if you please." Bradford cupped his nape, and pulled in a hefty expanse of air. "I hesitate to bring this up now, but I want to know, and I'm sure Philomena and Giles would as well."

"What is it, dear?" Aunt Muriel peered up at him, her expression open and inviting. She'd always been like that, never one to shy from the truth.

"Do you know why my uncle held the Pomfretts in such contempt? He was a self-seeking crotchety boor to all but an elite few, but his animosity toward them seemed beyond his normal spitefulness." He clasped Philomena's hand, needing to touch her, to reaffirm she was truly going to be his wife at long last.

Consternation swept his aunt's features as she slowly nodded. "It's an age old tale of thwarted love. He had a *tendre* for Mary Pomfrett, and when she publically chose a lowly vicar over him, well, it turned Herbert—always privileged and spoiled—into a bitter man."

"So rancorous he would deliberately set a fire to keep me from marrying Philomena? One that killed her parents and scarred her?" Bradford shook his head, unable to procure a speck of empathy or pity for the old viscount's plight. "Pray God forgave his acrimonious soul, for I shan't."

"Yes, even I struggle to believe he stooped to such unsavory methods." She opened the door, Olivia right behind her. "Don't bother to dress for dinner. Philomena, do you intend to join us, or would you prefer a tray in here?"

"A tray, I think, if you do not object." Regarding

her brother as he lay sleeping, Philomena's usually smooth brow furrowed. "I'll help feed Giles, too. Would you send Robins to sit with him for a spell first, though?"

While the maid monitored Giles, Bradford and Philomena had strolled in the quaint courtyard together every afternoon since her arrival, spending a pleasant half an hour reminiscing and renewing their friendship. He'd been hard-pressed to refrain from sweeping her into his arms and kissing her breathless each time, except that instinct warned she needed time to adjust.

"Certainly, my dear. I'll send her at once with fresh linens, too. Come along, Olivia. We've much to plan for your nuptials. I was pondering the menu for the wedding breakfast and ..." Sweeping from the room in a flurry of skirts, she continued to issue orders until the women were out of earshot.

Philomena stood and, after stretching her arms overhead, petted the cat whose contented rumbles increased in volume. "Doctor Singleton should be here shortly. If you don't mind, I should like to seek some air in the garden."

By herself?

Her falsely merry tone didn't fool Bradford. On the cusp of weeping, she sought privacy. Did she fear Giles wouldn't survive until she and Bradford had wed? Didn't she know he didn't give a tittle what the *ton* thought? They would be married straightaway, even if the unthinkable occurred, if Giles died, protocol be hanged.

He scooped the cat into his arms rather than crush Philomena to his chest and banish her fears. "A grand notion. I shall accompany you."

`   "There's no need," she demurred, her gaze cast to the floor.

Yes. By herself.

A kernel of an idea took root. "Why don't we go to Reverend Hawksworth, with a letter of introduction from Aunt Muriel? We would be gone an hour or two at most."

She touched a knuckle to the corner of an eye. "I ..."

Tears. Admirable, her self-control.

"I must speak with you." Seizing his arm, she

dragged him toward the open door.

Trepidation sank her talons deep. Philomena didn't want her brother overhearing whatever she had to say. Giles didn't stir as she towed Bradford along. Had he sunk into oblivion again or had the exhausted sleep of the ailing claimed him?

Closing the door behind them, Philomena canvassed the hallway. She clasped her hands beneath her chin and shut her eyelids, dragging in a ragged breath. Her lashes slowly eased open, her turbulent gaze a *mélange* of anguish and regret. "I'm not positive we should marry at all."

8

Guilt poked Philomena, its sharp little claws digging deep.

She must wed, to bring Giles peace, and she did love Bradford. Desperately. But so many things remained unresolved, not the least of which was whether Bradford could abide her scars.

If not, and he found her abhorrent, couldn't bear to touch her, then how would he beget an heir? He should see what he was getting before committing himself to a lifetime of regret. Well, she could insist he never see her naked, however, he didn't seem the sort to fumble under a nightgown in the dark, and she couldn't very well disrobe and let him gawk his fill before they wed.

A door shut along the corridor, and she wheeled around. This conversation wasn't meant for the servants' gossip fodder.

Robins, her arms full of linens, bustled their way, her white cap flopping up and down with her brisk pace. The maid grinned, her cheeks apple-plump and her owl-like gaze swinging between Philomena and Bradford. "Her grace said I was to sit with Mr. Pomfrett, and Peters and I are to change his sheets after he eats."

"Yes, please. I've asked for a tray to be brought up for him later. I'll be in my chamber or the garden should you need me." Philomena couldn't contain her ecstatic smile. "He awoke earlier and spoke."

"That's wonderful, miss." Robins moved to the entrance, and Bradford eased the door open and then stepped out of the way. "Thank you, my lord."

He angled his raven head in acknowledgement but remained silent as the maid disappeared inside, closing the door softly behind her. He extended an arm toward an oriel window. Dust particles danced in the sun rays shining through its floor-to-ceiling mullioned windows. "Let's move there, shall we? More private, I think, yet still respectable. Servants have been known to listen and peek through keyholes."

Their feet swishing softly on the plush Aubusson runner, they silently covered the short distance. Around a bend in the passageway, the recess wasn't visible from any bedchamber door.

Philomena faced Bradford and folded her hands before her. "I know I've shocked you, however, I have some reservations."

Shocked herself, truth to tell. Nonetheless, the unanswered questions and uncertainty had bubbled forth until she couldn't contain them any longer.

"Why? What are you afraid of?" Bradford regarded her silently, concern or curiosity, perhaps both, crinkling the corner of his eyes.

Giles dying.

Hastening into a marriage for the wrong reasons.

You finding my scars disgusting.

Biting her lip, Philomena breathed out a silent sigh. The reasons seemed trifling if spoken aloud, and chagrin taunted her because her love hadn't quashed every doubt. Shouldn't love do that? Plow aside hesitation and trepidation?

He gathered several tendrils of hair curling over her arm and, after rubbing them together, gave a slight tug. "Out with it. Tell me."

When he toyed with her hair, his fingertips caressing the strands, sensual musings of those long fingers elsewhere wreaked havoc with her concentration. Flinging her hair over her shoulder, she willed her romping pulse to behave itself. "I will not leave my brother under any circumstances. Not even for a wedding trip. And there's been no discussion of what happens to him if I marry. What's he to do? His care could be lengthy and costly."

Bradford's beautiful eyes widened, bemusement replacing the seductive glint. "Whether he lives a week, a year, or more, I never expected you to leave your brother. I would do the same if it were Olivia." A shock of hair had fallen onto his forehead, and his mouth lifted into a wry smile "In my eagerness to wed you, I've been remiss in explaining my thoughts, but I assure you, I assumed he would live with us for the remainder of his life, and I fully intend to pay for his needs. He'll be my family, too."

"Oh. I wasn't certain ..." Suddenly chilled, she wrapped her arms across her chest and clasped her shoulder. Giving him a shamefaced smile, she hitched a shoulder. "I confess to a fit of the nerves. I'm cold and my feet are freezing."

His attention sank to her scuffed half-boots.

"In those? Really? I can call for a hot brick and woolen stockings. A lap robe too." Giving her a devilishly provocative grin, he cocked an eyebrow and chucked her chin. "Or ... there are other, much more enjoyable, ways of warming you. We *are* betrothed ..."

At his allusion, a whorl of heat spread languidly through her veins. He'd always been able to do that, ease her fears and calm her with a few sensible words, as well as send her desires soaring. If only she possessed the pluck to snatch Bradford by his large hand and haul him into her bedchamber. She'd fantasized about lying with him for so long, she feared the real act might disappoint.

Rubbish. What she really feared was his reaction upon seeing her naked.

Sensibility reigned.

"No, you goose." *More's the pity*. Not until the vows are spoken. *If they're spoken.*

Philomena leaned against the wall beside the oriel. Careful not to bump the framed portrait of an intense looking fellow with a ruffled collar and neatly trimmed beard, hanging beside her, she tortured the edge of the

130

carpet with her boot.

"What else troubles you? I see it in your eyes, Philomena, the doubt and consternation." Joining her alongside the paneling, he positioned himself so his shoulder supported his weight. He traced her jaw, his eyes gleaming with longing. "I do love you, more with each passing day. More than I believed a human could love another."

"My scars ..." She released a puff of air and examined the cornice edging the ceiling. "They are quite unsightly. I fear after you see them, you'll not desire me anymore, not want to bed me, and that, in time, you'll grow bitter and resentful, that you'll grow to despise me."

Tenderly grasping her chin, he turned her face to his. "Never. Because it's you I love." He tapped her temple then her chest over her heart. "What's in there matters more than all else, though I find you tempting beyond reason, woman."

Cupping her ribs with his hands, he trailed hot kisses from below her ear to her shoulder.

God above.

She clamped onto his shoulders as sensation sluiced to every nerve. If his kisses did this to her, she'd shatter if they joined.

His breathing heavy and irregular, he pulled her tight against him and rocked his pelvis into her. A hard bump probed her belly. "Even if your entire body were scarred, you'd still do this to me. I love you. The rest matters naught."

Sincerity colored his words, but the look in his eyes, complete adoration, convinced her he spoke the truth. He did love her.

Others might not understand how quickly their love had rejuvenated, might hint it wasn't possible and that such unions only happened in fairy tales or silly novels, but Philomena knew what they had was real. And that's all that mattered, not whether anyone else believed it possible. Just as some people fell in love at first sight, others had a love like she and Bradford's. It would never die, not even when they breathed their last breath. Her spirit was tethered to his, and in the afterlife, they'd find one another and spend eternity together.

"I believe you." Philomena clasped her arms behind his back, basking in his love and caresses. She'd be an utter fool to forfeit this ... him. "And I love you, too."

With a final searing kiss, he leaned away. "Enough, or I won't be able to stop, and I'm positive tupping my future viscountess in full view of Berkeley Square would go down in history as a marked act of depravity." He winked and bobbed his head toward the window. "Although, I'd wager we'd draw quite a titillated audience."

The street outside bustled with activity. She giggled. "No doubt."

Bradford touched his pocket. "The license is good for three months. Why don't we take it one day at a time? I shall even court you, and you let me know when you are ready."

"No, we wanted to wait three weeks originally, but then Giles coughed up blood." She pushed away from the wall and snared his hand. "I don't want to wait that long."

Darting a quick look over the balustrade—no one lurked below listening to their conversation—she gave him what she hoped was an inviting smile. "Come."

Almost running the corridor's length, their hurried steps muffled by the plush carpet, she made straight for her bedchamber, a bemused Bradford unquestioningly allowing her to lug him along. As she reached for her door latch, misgiving again tried to raise its disagreeable head, but Philomena quelled it with a firm box to the ears.

She would know today which path providence had set her on, and it would be of her own making. Releasing Bradford's hand as she unlatched her door, she smiled over her shoulder.

"Lock it, will you?"

Not waiting for him to answer, she made straight for the ornate panel dressing screen with its charming cherub motif. She started slightly when the door's bolt slid home. Well, at least they wouldn't be walked in on. Most discomfiting that would be if her plans went as she hoped.

"What are you about?" He stood just inside the room, one hand on his slim hip and a crooked, sensual smile that suggested he knew precisely what she intended.

"You'll see."

Would he ever.

Flapping her hand at the overstuffed velvet armchair before the marble hearth, she squashed her romping nerves. Foreign to brazen and seductive conduct, she might very well come across as an inept trull with her first paying customer. "Please make yourself comfortable. I shall be but a few moments."

"That's the ugliest piece of furniture I have ever laid eyes upon." He strode to the chair and, after tossing aside a tasseled throw pillow, sat down.

She quite agreed. The burnt orange and moss green decor, as well as the cumbersome, carved furnishings reflected the duchess's bold taste.

Casting every misgiving aside—well, actually, she tromped atop their pointy little smirking heads— Philomena swept behind the screen. Taking a bracing breath, she bent to remove her footwear.

You can do this.

Faint rustling carried to her from beyond the screen. Bradford must have become restless and wandered the room. Perfectly wonderful. How soon before boredom prompted him to take his leave? She couldn't let him go.

Hurry!

Biting her lip, she tried to, but as often happens when one rushes, she possessed ten thumbs, each of which conspired to prevent her from removing her clothing.

"Dash it all," she mumbled into the dress's folds

wadded around her head.

"What's that?" His question sounded distant and muffled.

Was he leaving? No, by George.

Yanking the ribbon from her hair, and still wearing her chemise, she bolted from behind the screen, stubbing her toe on the panel's edge.

Curses.

"Bradford—" Tripping to an abrupt stop, jaw slack, she blinked in disbelief.

Bare-chested, the most tempting smattering of black, curly hair visible above the loudly-colored counterpane draped across his lap, he sat propped in her bed. He gave her a smoldering smile that sent tremors to her toes.

"I didn't think it fair that you should be the only one undressed."

She pressed her hands to the worst of her scars peeking above her lacy neckline. "Are you ... *naked?*"

"Indeed, though I'm wholly disappointed you are not. I'll admit, you are quite fetching in that filmy thing." He feigned a pout, which didn't deter his ravenous examination of her from toe to shoulder before returning to the dark tips showing through the chemise's thin fabric. Slowly, appreciation sharpening the lines of his face, he lifted his gaze to hers.

"Did I misunderstand?"

A jot of uncertainty tempered his voice.

"No. I'd hoped we would ..." Heat crept up her neck to her face. She likely glowed like a fire coal. "After I showed you my burns."

"Come here." He beckoned with one hand while patting the bed with the other.

The intensity of his gaze drew her forward until she stood beside the bed, afraid to look into his eyes, to see rejection there.

He touched the damaged flesh, the pads of his fingers tracing the burns, and she closed her eyes, to both relish in his caress and block out any disgust that might flit across his expression or spark in his eyes.

He whisked her chemise over her head, and she gasped against the rush of cold and abrupt vulnerability.

Refusing to open her eyes, she balled her hands and held her breath ... waiting.

"Philomena, look at me."

Bradford nudged her chin, and she stubbornly shook her head.

"Silly, love." He snaked a well-muscled arm around her waist and had her lying beside him before the air left her lungs in a startled squeak.

"These," he spread his hand over the thick, reddish marks crisscrossing her chest above her breasts, "make me adore you more. My heart, my very soul, aches for what you've suffered, but do not ever entertain the slightest notion that I would spurn you because of them."

A tear leaked from the corner of her eye, and she turned her head away from his tender expression. "They are ugly. I am ugly."

Her nakedness didn't embarrass her, but she found her scars mortifying. How could she expect him to become accustomed to their hideousness?

Bradford pressed his lips to the disfigurements. "I love you just as you are, whether unblemished or scarred. I want to make you my wife," he flattened his hand over her belly, "fill you with my children, and live every day as if it is our last. I'll never leave you again, never. You have to give me a chance to prove my love. Don't reject me, crush our happiness, and forgo our future out of fear. Please, trust me. "

Turning onto her side, Philomena searched his

face. Placing her hands on either side of his square jaw, she kissed him with all the pent-up longing and adoration she'd held in check. "I do trust you, and I do want to marry you."

He skimmed his hand the length of her rib, sending a myriad of sparks skittering across her. Squeezing a buttock, he kissed her forehead. "No more doubts?"

"Not a one." She pressed her mouth to the juncture of his throat and neck. His manly smell, slightly spicy but with a hint of musk and tobacco, enveloped her. Nuzzling his neck, she sniffed.

A deep rumble reverberated in his chest as he chuckled. "Here I am trying to seduce you, and you're sniffing me."

"Well, you smell wonderful." She grinned, giving him a coy look, and rested her chin on his chest. "It was I who set out to seduce you. Remember?"

A mock expression of horror swept his face. "Say it isn't so. My future viscountess is a seductress? How splendid."

He cupped her breast and captured her lips in a sizzling kiss.

Groaning, she squirmed, trying to get closer, to press her entire body against his skin. She kicked the sheets aside and leaned into his solid thighs and torso. Exploring his rigid muscles with inexperienced fingers, she mimicked the hot thrusting of his tongue. Her head swam with the force of her passion.

Three sharp raps interrupted their kiss.

Stiffening, Philomena tore her mouth from Bradford's, and he turned his head toward the door.

"Oh dear. I did tell Robins I'd be in my chamber," she whispered, shifting to rise. Bloody awkward, being caught abed by the maid.

"Bradford, Philomena, Reverend Hawksworth has arrived."

The duchess.

Philomena clapped her hand over her mouth and clobbered Bradford with a pillow when he chuckled.

"As luck would have it, he was at White's with Wimpleton." Aunt Muriel's voice shook suspiciously. "When you're finished, please meet us in the drawing room. Don't rush on our account. I've invited him to dinner, so you've plenty of time. Enjoy yourselves."

The duchess's delighted laughter echoed in the corridor.

"Good Lord. She knows." Philomena pressed her hands to her scorching face.

"That's that, then. We must wed at once now. I've utterly ruined you." Bradford pounced on her, pressing her back into the bedding and tickling her ribs.

Giggling, she gasped, "Not utterly, yet."

"Oh, trust me, woman." His hot gaze sank to her breasts. "I mean to compromise you beyond redemption."

Epilogue

Bromham Hall, England

August 1819

"**B**radford, look!" A series of stars whipped across the night sky. Philomena leapt from the settee, pointing. "Just like the night we were reunited."

She scooped her infant son from his cradle. Hurrying to the French windows—open to let in the evening's cool air—she kissed his downy head.

"See, Giles? Mama and Papa saw stars like this the night your Uncle Giles, smart man that he was, insisted we wed."

Bradford encircled her from behind and dropped a

kiss on her crown. "I owe your brother a debt I'll never be able to repay."

"The same is true of me." Lifting the gurgling infant, happily waving his tiny fists, she brushed her face against his soft, sweet-smelling cheek and closed her eyes. "At least he lived long enough to meet his namesake."

"A miracle, that. I didn't think he'd last the night after his collapse at Wimpleton's ball." He tightened his arms a fraction as he bent to bestow a kiss on their son. "His life was short, but at least his last days were peaceful and painless."

"I'm so grateful he didn't suffer."

Resting against Bradford, Philomena gazed at the clear sky, each star so vibrant, it seemed she could snatch it from the heavens. Another star whizzed past.

"See, there's another. Make a wish." Bradford nudged her head with his chin. "Hurry, before it's too late."

"What could I possibly wish for?" She slanted her head to look at him. "I am already blissfully content."

"Anything, my love." He kissed her nose. "It can

only be a boon to our happiness."

"Well, then, what I wish is to couple with you, every day, twice on Sundays, until I'm an ancient, shriveled crone." She chuckled at the image.

"That's a scandalous wish for a lady." He turned her in his embrace, and lowered his head. "But one I'm positive will come true, starting this very moment."

About the Author

USA Today Bestselling, award-winning author COLLETTE CAMERON® scribbles Scottish and Regency historicals featuring dashing rogues and scoundrels and the intrepid damsels who re-form them. Blessed with an overactive and witty muse that won't stop whispering new romantic romps in her ear, she's lived in Oregon her entire life, though she dreams of living in Scotland part-time. A self-confessed Cadbury chocoholic, you'll always find a dash of inspiration and a pinch of humor in her sweet-to-spicy timeless romances®.

Explore **Collette's worlds** at
www.collettecameron.com!

Join her **VIP Reader Club** and **FREE newsletter**.
Giggles guaranteed!

FREE BOOK: Join Collette's The Regency Rose®
VIP Reader Club to get updates on book releases,
cover reveals, contests and giveaways she reserves
exclusively for email and newsletter followers. Also,
any deals, sales, or special promotions are offered to
club members first. She will not share your name or
email, nor will she spam you.

http://bit.ly/TheRegencyRoseGift

Follow Collette on BookBub
https://www.bookbub.com/authors/collette-cameron

From the Desk of Collette Cameron

Dearest Reader,

I knew the minute I introduced Bradford in *A Kiss for a Rogue* that one day he'd get his own love story.

Readers adored him and kept asking me about him.

It was time to add another book to The Honorable Rogues® series. Naturally Bradford was my first choice for a hero, and so, *A Rogue's Scandalous Wish* came to be.

Philomena's character was tricky for me. A few years ago, I lost three family members in two separate house fires within ten months, and with a brother and brother-in-law who are fire chiefs (and a sister who is a fire captain) the whole issue of a heroine scarred by fire became very personal.

I hope you enjoy the telling of their story!

Please consider telling other readers why you

enjoyed this book by reviewing it. Not only do I truly want to hear your thoughts, reviews are crucial for an author to succeed. **Even if you only leave a line or two, I'd very much appreciate it.**

So, with that I'll leave you.

Here's wishing you many happy hours of reading, more happily ever afters than you can possibly enjoy in a lifetime, and abundant blessings to you and your loved-ones.

Collette Cameron

A Kiss for a Rogue

The Honorable Rogues™, Book One

Formerly titled A Kiss for Miss Kingsley

**A lonely wallflower. A future viscount.
A second chance at love.**

Olivia Kingsley didn't expect to be swept off her feet and receive a marriage proposal two weeks into her first Season. However, one delicious dance with Allen Wimpleton, and her future is sealed. Or so she thinks until her eccentric father suddenly announces he's moving the family to the Caribbean for a year.

Terrified of losing Olivia, Allen begs her to elope, but she refuses. Distraught at her leaving, and unaware of her father's ill-health, Allen doubts her love and foolishly demands she choose—him or her father.

Heartbroken at his callousness, Olivia turns her back on their love. The year becomes three, enough time for her broken heart to heal, and after her father dies, she returns to England.

Coming face to face with Allen at a ball, she realizes she never purged him from her heart.

But can they overcome their pasts and old wounds to trust love again? Or has Allen found another in her absence?

Enjoy the first chapter of

A Kiss for a Rogue

The Honorable Rogues®, Book One

A lady must never forget her
manners nor lose her composure.
~*A Lady's Guide to Proper Comportment*

London, England
Late May, 1818

"This is a monumental mistake."

*God's toenails. What were you thinking,
Olivia Kingsley, agreeing to Auntie Muriel's
addlepated scheme?*

Why had she ever agreed to this farce?

Fingering the heavy ruby pendant hanging at the

hollow of her neck, Olivia peeked out the window as the conveyance rounded the corner onto Berkeley Square. Good God. Carriage upon carriage, like great shiny beetles, lined the street beside an ostentatious manor. Her heart skipped a long beat, and she ducked out of sight.

Braving another glance from the window's corner, her stomach pitched worse than a ship amid a hurricane. The full moon's milky light, along with the mansion's rows of glowing diamond-shaped panes, illuminated the street. Dignified guests in their evening finery swarmed before the grand entrance and on the granite stairs as they waited their turn to enter Viscount and Viscountess Wimpleton's home.

The manor had acquired a new coat of paint since she had seen it last. She didn't care for the pale lead shade, preferring the previous color, a pleasant, welcoming bronze green. Why anyone living in Town would choose to wrap their home in such a chilly color was beyond her. With its enshrouding fog and perpetually overcast skies, London boasted every shade of gray already.

Three years in the tropics, surrounded by vibrant flowers, pristine powdery beaches, a turquoise sea, and balmy temperatures had rather spoiled her against London's grime and stench. How long before she grew accustomed to the dank again? The gloom? The smell?

Never.

Shivering, Olivia pulled her silk wrap snugger. Though late May, she'd been nigh on to freezing since the ship docked last week.

A few curious guests turned to peer in their carriage's direction. A lady swathed in gold silk and dripping diamonds, spoke into her companion's ear and pointed at the gleaming carriage. Did she suspect someone other than Aunt Muriel sat behind the distinctive Daventry crest?

Trepidation dried Olivia's mouth and tightened her chest. Would many of the *ton* remember her?

Stupid question, that. Of course she would be remembered.

Much like ivy—its vines clinging tenaciously to a tree—or a barnacle cemented to a rock, one couldn't easily be pried from the upper ten thousand's memory.

But, more on point, would anyone recall her fascination with Allen Wimpleton?

Inevitably.

Coldness didn't cause the new shudder rippling from her shoulder to her waist.

Yes. Attending the ball was a featherbrained solicitation for disaster. No good could come of it. Flattening against the sky-blue and gold-trimmed velvet squab in the corner of her aunt's coach, Olivia vehemently shook her head.

"I cannot do it. I thought I could, but I positively cannot."

A curl came loose, plopping onto her forehead.

Bother.

The dratted, rebellious nuisance that passed for her hair escaped its confines more often than not. She shoved the annoying tendril beneath a pin, having no doubt the tress would work its way free again before evenings end. Patting the circlet of rubies adorning her hair, she assured herself the band remained secure. The treasure had belonged to Aunt Muriel's mother, a Prussian princess, and no harm must come to it.

Olivia's pulse beat an irregular staccato as she searched for a plausible excuse for refusing to attend the ball after all. She wouldn't lie outright, which ruled out her initial impulse to claim a *megrim*.

"I ... we—" She wiggled her white-gloved fingers at her brother, lounging on the opposite seat. "Were not invited."

Contented as their fat cat, Socrates, after lapping a saucer of fresh cream, Bradford settled his laughing gaze on her. "Yes, we mustn't do anything untoward."

Terribly vulgar, that. Arriving at a *haut ton* function, no invitation in hand. She and Bradford mightn't make it past the vigilant majordomo, and then what were they to do? Scuttle away like unwanted pests? Mortifying and prime tinder for the gossips.

"Whatever will people *think*?" Bradford thrived on upending Society. If permitted, he would dance naked as a robin just to see the reactions. He cocked a cinder-black brow, his gray-blue eyes holding a challenge.

Toad.

Olivia yearned to tell him to stop giving her that loftier look. Instead, she bit her tongue to keep from sticking it out at him like she had as a child. Irrationality warred with reason, until her common sense finally prevailed. "I wouldn't want to impose, is all I meant."

"Nonsense, darling. It's perfectly acceptable for you and Bradford to accompany me." The seat creaked as Aunt Muriel, the Duchess of Daventry, bent forward to scrutinize the crowd. She patted Olivia's knee. "Lady Wimpleton is one of my dearest friends. Why, we had our come-out together, and I'm positive had she known that you and Bradford had recently returned to England, she would have extended an invitation herself."

Olivia pursed her lips.

Not if she knew the volatile way her son and I parted company, she wouldn't have.

A powerful peeress, few risked offending Aunt Muriel, and she knew it well. She could haul a haberdasher or a milkmaid to the ball and everyone would paste artificial smiles on their faces and bid the duo a pleasant welcome. Reversely, if someone earned her scorn, they had best pack-up and leave London permanently before doors began slamming in their faces. Her influence rivaled that of the Almack's patronesses.

Bradford shifted, presenting Olivia with his striking profile as he, too, took in the hubbub before the manor. "You will never be at peace—never be able to move on—unless you do this."

That morsel of knowledge hadn't escaped her, which was why she had agreed to the scheme to begin with. Nevertheless, that didn't make seeing Allen Wimpleton again any less nerve-wracking.

"You must go in, Livy," Bradford urged, his countenance now entirely brotherly concern.

She stopped plucking at her mantle and frowned. "Please don't call me that, Brady."

Once, a lifetime ago, Allen had affectionately called her Livy—until she had refused to succumb to his begging and run away to Scotland. Regret momentarily altered her heart rhythm.

Bradford hunched one of his broad shoulders and scratched his eyebrow. "What harm can come of it? We'll only stay as long as you like, and I promise, I shall remain by your side the entire time."

Their aunt's unladylike snort echoed throughout the carriage.

"And the moon only shines in the summer." Her voice dry as desert sand, and skepticism peaking her eyebrows high on her forehead, Aunt Muriel fussed with her gloves. "Nephew, I have never known you to forsake an opportunity to become, er ..."

She slid Olivia a guarded glance. "Shall we say, become better acquainted with the ladies? This Season, there are several tempting beauties and a particularly large assortment of amiable young widows eager for a *distraction*."

Did Aunt Muriel truly believe Olivia don't know about Bradford's reputation with females? She was neither blind nor ignorant.

He turned and flashed their aunt one of his dazzling smiles, his deeply tanned face making it all the more brighter. "All pale in comparison to you two lovelies, no doubt."

Olivia made an impolite noise and, shaking her head, aimed her eyes heavenward in disbelief.

Doing it much too brown. Again.

Bradford was too charming by far—one reason the fairer sex were drawn to him like ants to molasses. She'd been just as doe-eyed and vulnerable when it came to Allen.

"Tish tosh, young scamp. Your compliments are wasted on me." Still, Aunt Muriel slanted her head, a pleased smile hovered on her lightly-painted mouth and pleating the corners of her eyes. "Besides, if you attach yourself to your sister, she won't have an opportunity to find herself alone with young Wimpleton."

Olivia managed to keep her jaw from unhinging as she gaped at her aunt. She snapped her slack mouth shut with an audible click. "Shouldn't you be cautioning me *not* to be alone with a gentleman?"

Aunt Muriel chuckled and patted Olivia's knee again. "That rather defeats the purpose in coming tonight then, doesn't it, dear?" Giving a naughty wink, she nudged Olivia. "I do hope Wimpleton kisses you. He's such a handsome young man. Quite the Corinthian too."

A hearty guffaw escaped Bradford, and he slapped his knee. "Aunt Muriel, I refuse to marry until I find a female as colorful as you. Life would never be dull."

"I should say not. Daventry and I had quite the adventurous life. It's in my blood, you know, and yours too, I suspect. Papa rode his stallion right into a church and actually snatched Mama onto his lap moments before she was forced to marry an abusive lecher. The scandal, they say, was utterly delicious." The duchess sniffed, a put-upon expression on her lined face. "Dull indeed. *Hmph*. Never. Why, I may have to be vexed with you the entire evening for even hinting such a preposterous thing."

"Grandpapa abducted Grandmamma? In church, no less?" Bradford dissolved into another round of hearty laughter, something he did often as evidenced by the lines near his eyes.

Unable to utter a single sensible rebuttal, Olivia swung her gaze between them. Her aunt and brother beamed, rather like two naughty imps, not at all abashed at having been caught with their mouth's full of stolen sweetmeats from the kitchen.

She wrinkled her nose and gave a dismissive flick of her wrist. "Bah. You two are completely hopeless where decorum is concerned."

"Don't mistake decorum for stodginess or pomposity, my dear." Her aunt gave a sage nod. "Neither permits a mite of fun and both make one a cantankerous boor."

Bradford snickered again, his hair, slightly too long for London, brushing his collar. "By God, if only there were more women like you."

Olivia itched to box his ears. Did he take nothing seriously?

No. Not since Philomena had died.

Olivia edged near the window once more and worried the flesh of her lower lip. Carriages continued to line up, two or three abreast. Had the entire *beau monde* turned out for the grand affair?

Botheration. Why must the Wimpletons be so well-received?

She caught site of her tense face reflected in the glass, and hastily turned away.

"And, Aunt Muriel, you're absolutely positive that

Allen—that is, Mr. Wimpleton—remains unattached?"

Fiddling with her shawl's silk fringes, Olivia attempted a calming breath. No force on heaven or earth could compel her to enter the manor if Allen were betrothed or married to another. Her fragile heart, though finally mended after three years of painful healing, could bear no more anguish or regret.

If he were pledged to another, she would simply take the carriage back to Aunt Muriel's, pack her belongings, and make for Bromham Hall, Bradford's newly inherited country estate. Olivia would make a fine spinster; perhaps even take on the task of housekeeper in order to be of some use to her brother. She would never set foot in Town again.

She dashed her aunt an impatient, sidelong peek. Why didn't Aunt Muriel answer the question?

Head to the side and eyes brimming with compassion, Aunt Muriel regarded her.

"You're certain he's not courting anyone?" Olivia pressed for the truth. "There's no one he has paid marked attention to? You must tell me, mustn't fear for my sensibilities or that I'll make a scene."

She didn't make scenes.

The *A Lady's Guide to Proper Comportment* was most emphatic in that regard.

Only the most vulgar and lowly bred indulge in histrionics or emotional displays.

Aunt Muriel shook her turbaned head firmly. The bold ostrich feather topping the hair covering jolted violently, and her diamond and emerald cushion-shaped earrings swung with the force of her movement. She adjusted her gaudily-colored shawl.

"No. No one. Not from the lack of enthusiastic mamas, and an audacious papa or two, shoving their simpering daughters beneath his nose, I can tell you. Wimpleton's considered a brilliant catch, quite dashing, and a top-sawyer, to boot." She winked wickedly again. "Why, if I were only a score of years younger ..."

"Yes? What *would* you do, Aunt Muriel?" Rubbing his jaw, Bradford grinned.

Olivia flung him a flinty-eyed glare. "Hush. Do not encourage her."

Worse than children, the two of them.

Lips pursed, Aunt Muriel ceased fussing with her skewed pendant and tapped her fingers upon her plump thigh. "I would wager a year's worth of my favorite pastries that fast Rossington chit has set her cap for him, though. Has her feline claws dug in deep, too, I fear."

A Bride for a Rogue

The Honorable Rogues®, Book Two

Formerly titled Bride of Falcon

**She can't forget the past. He can't face the future.
Until fate intervenes one night.**

Many years ago, Ivonne Wimpleton loved Chancy Faulkenhurst and hoped to marry him. Then one day, without any explanation, he sailed to India. Now, after five unsuccessful Seasons and a riding accident that left her with a slight limp, her only suitors are fortune-hunters and degenerates. Just as Ivy's resigned herself to spinsterhood, Chance unexpectedly returns.

Upon returning to England, Chance is disillusioned, disfigured, and emotionally scarred, but his love for Ivy remains is strong. However, he's failed to acquire the fortune he sought in order to earn permission to marry her. When he discovers Ivy's being forced to wed to prevent a scandalous secret from being revealed, he's determined to make her his bride.

Except, believing Chance made no effort to contact her all those years, Ivy's furious with him. What's more, in his absence, his father arranged a profitable marriage for Chance. As he battles his own inner demons, he must convince Ivy to risk loving him again. But will their parents' interference jeopardize Chance and Ivy's happiness once more?

To Capture a Rogue's Heart

The Honorable Rogues®, Book Four

Formerly titled To Tame a Scoundrel's Heart

He recruited her to help him find a wife…
…and discovered she was the perfect candidate.

Her betrothed cheated on her.

Katrina Needham intended to marry her beloved major and live happily-ever-after—until he's seen with another woman. Distraught, and needing a distraction, she agrees to assist the rugged, and dangerously handsome Captain Dominic St. Monté find a wife. So why does she find herself entertaining romantic notions about the privateer turned duke?

He believed he was illegitimate.

When Nic unexpectedly inherits a dukedom and the care of his young sisters, he reluctantly decides he must marry. Afterward, if his new duchess is willing, he hopes to return to the sea-faring life he craves part-time. If she doesn't agree, he'll have no choice but to give up the sea forever.

Will they forsake everything for each other?
Nic soon realizes Katrina possesses every characteristic he seeks in a duchess. The more time he spends with the vivacious beauty, the more enamored he becomes. Still, he cannot ask for her hand. Not only is she still officially promised to another, she has absolutely no interest in becoming a duchess, much less a privateer's wife.

Can Nic and Katrina relinquish their carefully planned futures and trust love to guide them?

The Rogue and the Wallflower

The Honorable Rogues®, Book Five

Formerly titled The Wallflower's Wicked Wager

He loved her beyond anything and everything—precisely why he must never marry her.

Love—sentimental drivel for weak, feckless fools.
Since an explosion ravaged Captain Morgan Le Draco's face and cost him his commission in the Royal Dragoons, he's fortified himself behind a rampart of cynicism and distrust. He's put aside all thoughts of marrying until he risks his life to save a drowning woman. At once, Morgan knows Shona's the balm for his tortured soul. But as a wealthy noblewoman, she's far above his humble station and can never be his.

Love—a treasured gift reserved for those beautiful of form and face.
Scorned and ridiculed most of her adult life, Shona Atterberry believes she's utterly undesirable and is reconciled to spinsterhood. She hides her spirited

temperament beneath a veneer of shyness. Despite how ill-suited they are, and innuendos that Captain Le Draco is a fortune-hunter, she cannot escape her growing fascination.

Two damaged souls searching for love.
Shona is goaded into placing a wicked wager. One that sets her upon a ruinous path and alienates the only man who might have ever loved her. Is true love enough to put their pasts behind them, to learn to trust, and to heal their wounded hearts.

The Earl and the Spinster

The Blue Rose Regency Romances:
The Culpepper Misses, Book One

Formerly titled Brooke: Wagers Gone Awry

**An angry earl. A desperate spinster.
A reckless wager.**

For five years, Brooke Culpepper has focused her energy on two things: keeping the struggling dairy farm that's her home operating and preventing her younger sister and cousins from starving. Then one day, a stern-faced stranger arrives at their doorstep and announces he's the dairy's new owner and plans on selling the farm. Though she's outraged, Brooke can't deny the Earl of Ravensdale makes her pulse race in the most disturbing way.

Heath is incensed to discover five women call the land he won at the gaming tables their home. He detests everything about the country and has no desire to own a smelly farm, even if one of the occupants is the most intelligent, entrancing woman he's ever met.

Desperate, pauper poor, and with nowhere to take her family, Brooke rashly proposes a wager. Heath's stakes? The farm. Hers? Her virtue. The land holds no interest for Heath, but he finds Brooke irresistible, and ignoring prudence as well as his sense of honor, he just as recklessly accepts her challenge.

In a winner-takes-all bet, will they both come to regret their impulsiveness, especially when love is at stake?

Enjoy the first chapter of

The Earl and the Spinster

The Blue Rose Regency Romances:
The Culpepper Misses, Book One

Even when most prudently considered,
and with the noblest of intentions, one who
wagers with chance oft finds oneself empty-handed.
~Wisdom and Advice
The Genteel Lady's Guide to Practical Living

Esherton Green,
Near Acton, Cheshire, England
Early April 1822

*W*as I born under an evil star or cursed from my
first breath?

Brooke Culpepper suppressed the urge to shake
her fist at the heavens and berate The Almighty aloud.

The devil boasted better luck than she. My God, now two *more* cows struggled to regain their strength?

She slid Richard Mabry, Esherton Green's steward-turned-overseer, a worried glance from beneath her lashes as she chewed her lower lip and paced before the unsatisfactory fire in the study's hearth. The soothing aroma of wood smoke, combined with linseed oil, old leather, and the faintest trace of Papa's pipe tobacco, bathed the room. The scents reminded her of happier times but did little to calm her frayed nerves.

Sensible gray woolen skirts swishing about her ankles, she whirled to make the return trip across the once-bright green and gold Axminster carpet, now so threadbare, the oak floor peeked through in numerous places. Her scuffed half-boots fared little better, and she hid a wince when the scrap of leather she'd used to cover the hole in her left sole this morning slipped loose again.

From his comfortable spot in a worn and faded wingback chair, Freddy, her aged Welsh corgi, observed her progress with soulful brown eyes, his muzzle propped on stubby paws. Two ancient tabbies lay curled so tightly together on the cracked leather sofa that determining where one ended and the other began was difficult.

What was she to do? Brooke clamped her lip harder and winced.

Should she venture to the barn to see the cows herself?

What good would that do? She knew little of doctoring cattle and so left the animals' care in Mr. Mabry's capable hands. Her strength lay in the financial administration of the dairy farm and her ability to stretch a shilling as thin as gossamer.

She cast a glance at the bay window and, despite the fire, rubbed her arms against the chill creeping along her spine. A frenzied wind whipped the lilac branches and scraped the rain-splattered panes. The tempest threatening since dawn had finally unleashed its full fury, and the fierce winds battering the house gave the day a peculiar, eerie feeling—as if portending something ominous.

At least Mabry and the other hands had managed to get the cattle tucked away before the gale hit. The herd of fifty—no, sixty, counting the newborn calves—chewed their cud and weathered the storm inside the old, but sturdy, barns.

As she peered through the blurry pane, a shingle ripped loose from the farthest outbuilding—a retired stone dovecote. After the wind tossed the slat around for a few moments, the wood twirled to the ground, where it flipped end over end before wedging beneath a gangly shrub. Two more shingles hurled to the earth, this time from one of the barns.

Flimflam and goose-butt feathers.

Brooke tamped down a heavy sigh. Each structure on the estate, including the house, needed some sort of repair or replacement: roofs, shutters, stalls, floors, stairs, doors, siding...dozens of items required fixing, and she could seldom muster the funds to go about it properly.

"Another pair of cows struggling, you say, Mr.

Mabry?"

Concern etched on his weathered features, Mabry wiped rain droplets from his face as water pooled at his muddy feet.

"Yes, Miss Brooke. The four calves born this mornin' fare well, but two of the cows, one a first-calf heifer, aren't standin' yet. And there's one weak from birthin' her calf yesterday." His troubled gaze strayed to the window. "Two more ladies are in labor. I best return to the barn. They seemed fine when I left, but I'd as soon be nearby."

Brooke nodded once. "Yes, we mustn't take any chances."

The herd had already been reduced to a minimum by disease and sales to make ends meet. She needed every shilling the cows' milk brought. Losing another, let alone two or three good breeders...

No, I won't think of it.

She stopped pacing and forced a cheerful smile. Nonetheless, from the skeptical look Mabry speedily masked, his thoughts ran parallel to hers—one reason she put her trust in the man. Honest and intelligent, he'd worked alongside her to restore the beleaguered herd and farm after Papa died. Their existence, their livelihood, everyone at Esherton's future depended on the estate flourishing once more.

"It's only been a few hours." *Almost nine, truth to tell.* Brooke scratched her temple. "Perhaps the ladies need a little more time to recover." *If they recovered.* "The calves are strong, aren't they?" *Please, God, they must be.* She held her breath, anticipating Mabry's response.

His countenance lightened and the merry sparkle returned to his eyes. "Aye, the mites are fine. Feedin' like they're hollow to their wee hooves."

Tension lessoned its ruthless grip, and hope peeked from beneath her vast mound of worries.

Six calves had been guaranteed in trade to her neighbor and fellow dairy farmer, Silas Huffington, for the grain and medicines he'd provided to see Esherton Green's herd through last winter. Brooke didn't have the means to pay him if the calves didn't survive—

though the old reprobate had hinted he'd make her a deal of a much less respectable nature if she ran short of cattle with which to barter. Each pence she'd stashed away—groat by miserable groat, these past four years—lay in the hidden drawer of Papa's desk and must go to purchase a bull.

Wisdom had decreed replacing Old Buford two years ago but, short on funds, she'd waited until it was too late. His heart had stopped while he performed the duties expected of a breeding bull. Not the worst way to cock up one's toes...er, hooves, but she'd counted on him siring at least two-score calves this season and wagered everything on the calving this year and next. The poor brute had expired before he'd completed the job.

Her thoughts careened around inside her skull. Without a bull, she would lose everything.

My home, care of my sister and cousins, my reasons for existing.

She squared her shoulders, resolution strengthening her. She still retained the Culpepper sapphire parure set. If all else failed, she would pawn the jewelry. She'd planned on using the money from the gems' sale to bestow small marriage settlements on the girls. Still, pawning the set was a price worth paying to keep her family at Esherton Green, even if it meant that any chance of her sister and three cousins securing a decent match would evaporate faster than a dab of milk on a hot cook stove. Good standing and breeding meant little if one's fortune proved meaner than a churchyard beggar's.

"How's the big bull calf that came breech on Sunday?" Brooke tossed the question over her shoulder as she poked the fire and encouraged the blaze to burn hotter. After setting the tool aside, she faced the overseer.

"Greediest of the lot." Mabry laughed and slapped his thigh. "Quite the appetite he has, and friendly as our Freddy there. Likes his ears scratched too."

Brooke chuckled and ran her hand across Freddy's spine. The dog wiggled in excitement and stuck his rear legs straight out behind him, gazing at her in adoration. In his youth, he'd been an excellent cattle herder. Now he'd gone fat and arthritic, his sweet face gray to his eyebrows. On occasion, he still dashed after the cattle, the instinctive drive to herd deep in the marrow of his bones.

Another shudder shook her. Why was she so blasted cold today? She relented and placed a good-sized log atop the others. The feeble flames hissed and spat before greedily engulfing the new addition. Lord, she prayed she wasn't ailing. She simply couldn't afford to become ill.

A scratching at the door barely preceded the entrance of Duffen bearing a tea service. "Gotten to where a man cannot find a quiet corner to shut his eyes for a blink or two anymore."

Shuffling into the room, he yawned and revealed how few teeth remained in his mouth. One sock sagged around his ankle, his grizzled hair poked every which way, and his shirttail hung askew. Typical Duffen.

"Devil's day, it is." He scowled in the window's direction, his mouth pressed into a grim line. "Mark my words, trouble's afoot.''

Not quite a butler, but certainly more than a simple retainer, the man, now hunched from age, had been a fixture at Esherton Green Brooke's entire life. He loved the place as much as, if not more than, she, and she couldn't afford to hire a servant to replace him. A light purse had forced Brooke to let the household staff go when Papa died. The cook, Mrs. Jennings, Duffen, and Flora, a maid-of-all-work, had stayed on. However, they received no salaries—only room and board.

The income from the dairy scarcely permitted Brooke to retain a few milkmaids and stable hands, yet not once had she heard a whispered complaint from anyone.

Everybody, including Brooke, her sister, Brette, and their cousins—Blythe, and the twins, Blaike and Blaire—did their part to keep the farm operating at a profit. A meager profit, particularly as, for the past five years, Esherton Green's legal heir, Sheridan Gainsborough, had received half the proceeds. In return, he permitted Brooke and the girls to reside there. He'd also been appointed their guardian. But, from his silence and failure to visit the farm, he seemed perfectly content to let her carry on as provider and caretaker.

"Ridiculous law. Only the next male in line can inherit," she muttered.

Especially when he proved a disinterested bore. Papa had thought so too, but the choice hadn't been his to make. If only she could keep the funds she sent to Sheridan each quarter, Brooke could make something of Esherton and secure her sister and cousins' futures too.

If wishes were gold pieces, I'd be rich indeed.

Brooke sneezed then sneezed again. Dash it all. A cold?

The fresh log snapped loudly, and Brooke started. The blaze's heat had failed to warm her opinion of her second cousin. She hadn't met him and lacked a personal notion of his character, but Papa had hinted that Sheridan was a scallywag and possessed unsavory habits.

A greedy sot, too.

The one time her quarterly remittance had been late, because Brooke had taken a tumble and broken her arm, he'd written a disagreeable letter demanding his money.

His money, indeed.

Sheridan had threatened to sell Esherton Green's acreage and turn her and the foursome onto the street if she ever delayed payment again.

A ruckus beyond the entrance announced the girls' arrival. Laughing and chatting, the blond quartet billowed into the room. Their gowns, several seasons out of fashion, in no way detracted from their charm, and pride swelled in Brooke's heart. Lovely, both in countenance and disposition, and the dears worked hard too.

"Duffen says we're to have tea in here today." Attired in a Pomona green gown too short for her tall frame, Blaike plopped on to the sofa. Her twin, Blaire, wearing a similar dress in dark rose and equally inadequate in length, flopped beside her.

Each girl scooped a drowsy cat into her lap. The cats' wiry whiskers twitched, and they blinked their sleepy amber eyes a few times before closing them once more as the low rumble of contented purrs filled the room.

"Yes, I didn't think we needed to light a fire in the drawing room when this one will suffice." As things stood, too little coal and seasoned firewood remained to see them comfortably until summer.

Brette sailed across the study, her slate-blue gingham dress the only one of the quartet's fashionably long enough. Repeated laundering had turned the garment a peculiar greenish color, much like tarnished copper. She looped her arm through Brooke's.

"Look, dearest." Brette pointed to the tray. "I splurged and made a half-batch of shortbread biscuits. It's been so long since we've indulged, and today is your birthday. To celebrate, I insisted on fresh tea leaves as well."

Brooke would have preferred to ignore the day.

Three and twenty.

On the shelf. Past her prime. Long in the tooth. Spinster. *Old maid.*

She'd relinquished her one chance at love. In order to nurse her ailing father and assume the care of her young sister and three orphaned cousins, she'd refused Humphrey Benbridge's proposal. She couldn't have put her happiness before their welfare and deserted them when they needed her most. Who would've cared for them if she hadn't?

No one.

Mr. Benbridge controlled the purse strings, and Humphrey had neither offered nor been in a position to take on their care. Devastated, or so he'd claimed, he'd departed to the continent five years ago.

She'd not seen him since.

Nonetheless, his sister, Josephina, remained a friend and occasionally remarked on Humphrey's travels abroad. Burying the pieces of her broken heart beneath hard work and devotion to her family, Brooke had rolled up her sleeves and plunged into her forced role as breadwinner, determined that sacrificing her love not be in vain.

Yes, it grieved her that she wouldn't experience a man's passion or bear children, but to wallow in doldrums was a waste of energy and emotion. Instead, she focused on building a future for her sister and cousins—so they might have what she never would—and allowed her dreams to fade into obscurity.

"Happy birthday." Brette squeezed her hand.

Brooke offered her sister a rueful half-smile. "Ah, I'd hoped you'd forgotten."

"Don't be silly, Brooke. We couldn't forget your special day." Twenty-year-old Blythe—standing with her hands behind her—grinned and pulled a small, neatly-wrapped gift tied with a cheerful yellow ribbon from behind her. Sweet dear. She'd used the trimming from her gown to adorn the package.

"Hmph. Need seedcake an' champagne to celebrate a birthday properly." The contents of the tray rattled and clanked when Duffen scuffed his way to the table between the sofa and chairs. After depositing the tea service, he lifted a letter from the surface. Tea dripped from one stained corner. "This arrived for you yesterday, Miss Brooke. I forgot where I'd put it until just now."

If I can read it with the ink running to London and back.

He shook the letter, oblivious to the tawny droplets spraying every which way.

Mabry raised a bushy gray eyebrow, and the twins hid giggles by concealing their faces in the cat's striped coats.

Brette set about pouring the tea, although her lips twitched suspiciously.

Freddy sat on his haunches and barked, his button eyes fixed on the paper, evidently mistaking it for a tasty morsel he would've liked to sample. He licked his chops, a testament to his waning eyesight.

"Thank you, Duffen." Brooke took the letter by one soggy corner. Holding it gingerly, she flipped it over. No return address.

"Aren't you going to read it?" Blythe set the gift

on the table before settling on the sofa and smoothing her skirt. They didn't get a whole lot of post at Esherton. Truth be known, this was the first letter in months. Blythe's gaze roved to the other girls and the equally eager expressions on their faces. "We're on pins and needles," she quipped, fluttering her hands and winking.

Brooke smiled and cracked the brownish wax seal with her fingernail. Their lives had become rather monotonous, so much so that a simple, *soggy*, correspondence sent the girls into a dither of anticipation.

My Dearest Cousin...

Brooke glanced up. "It's from Sheridan.

Made in the USA
Coppell, TX
15 March 2022

75000057R00115